Yorkshi

Shor Volume Two

Edited by

Joan Thornton
Olive Fowler &
Michael Yates

Everyone has a story
to tell. We find
ways of helping
them tell it.

Yorkshire Art Circus
1992

Published by Yorkshire Art Circus
School Lane, Glass Houghton, Castleford
West Yorkshire WF10 4QH
Telephone (0977) 550401

© Yorkshire Art Circus Ltd 1992
© Cover illustration and design by Tadpole Graphics
Typeset by: Yorkshire Art Circus Ltd
Printed by: Thornton & Pearson, Rosse Street,
                    Thornton Road, Bradford, BD8 9AS

ISBN 0 947780 79 3
Classification: fiction

Yorkshire Art Circus is a unique book publisher. We work to
increase access to writing and publishing and to develop new
models of practice for arts in the community.

For details of our full programme of workshops and our current
book list please write to the address above.

Yorkshire Art Circus is a registered charity (number 1007443)

Acknowledgements:

Rachel Adam   Pam Davenport
Andrea Richardson   Reini Schühle

**We would like to thank the following organisations for support
towards this book:**

Introduction

Short stories have always been popular with readers and writers alike. It's easy to see why. There is a neatness and simplicity in a good short story that engages the attention of the reader and leads swiftly to a satisfying resolution. Equally, writers who feel the need to encapsulate a particular experience find the form compulsively attractive.

The anthology, *Yorkshire Mixture,* provides an outlet for writers of short fiction - many of whom have never been published before.

From the familiar settings, from the little tricks of speech, from the common memories, we recognise the Yorkshire we live in. But we recognise also that the emotions, the conflicts and the humour have a much wider relevance. These stories - sometimes large in theme, sometimes trivial - deal with a universal experience.

Contents

My Prince

Stephen Davenport

I HAD a few fantasies to help speed the trudge of my paper round. One of them was to trot out of the Wembley tunnel in the all-white strip of Leeds United whilst modestly avoiding eye contact with the television cameras, another was to own a dog. I'd written to Leeds requesting a trial, but I hadn't thought it was worth asking if we could have a dog. Helen, one of my sisters, had already made that mistake. She was only seven but she'd had the sense to wait until my mum had inhaled a couple of lungfuls of her post-teatime Number 6, before nervously enquiring,

'Mummy?'

'Whatty?'

'Could we get a Yorkshire Terrier one day?'

Mum looked up irritably from Mary Marryat Advises in her Woman's Weekly.

'Course we can, why didn't you ask before?' She began shaping the red end of her fag in the ashtray, a sure sign she was building on the sarcastic theme.

'Tell you what, we'll get two. They'll be company for each other. I mean, I haven't got enough to do running round after five kids - if we have some mutt crapping all over the carpet, that'll really keep me on my toes, won't it?'

That had been that until one sunny Sunday in March 1973 during Three-Way Family Favourites. We'd just had our dinner when my dad appeared from behind the Sunday Express, custard specks glistening in his beard, and said, 'If we were to get a dog, would you all help your mum to look after it?'

'Great. Yes, Daddy.'

'Can we have a Yorkshire Terrier, please? I'll clean the carpet.'

'It's an Alsatian, and don't thank me, thank your mother. Frankly, she wasn't keen on the idea, but I managed to talk her round, didn't I, love?' Mum nodded, wearily forcing a smile. He had some good patter, did my dad.

He was driving taxis then. It had been Prince's job to guard the Morris Oxfords down at the mechanics' workshop. For three years he'd performed his duties inadvertently well. His joyous welcoming whoops and barks on hearing any human had probably scared off a few would-be casual intruders, but anyone with their wits about them couldn't help noticing that friendly great tail beating out a 'play with me' tattoo on car panels and anything else it thumped. One Monday morning, the mechanics arrived at work to be greeted by Prince with his huge head sticking through an open window. Inside, a brand new camshaft had gone walkies, so Prince lost a job and gained his freedom.

When we went to collect him, he was so filthy that my dad wouldn't have him in the car. 'Right,' said Dad, 'you're so bloody keen on having a dog, you can walk him back.' With that, he whipped out his penknife, hacked someone's washing line from the end of a terrace and slipped it round the dog's choker.

Two miles I had to walk him and I don't mind admitting I was worried, despite the tales about how soft he was. All went well for the first half-mile or so. I reeled him in as close as six feet to me when crossing roads, then played him out to fully fifteen feet when we hit the new estate. Just outside the Spar shop, I was hoisted by my own washing line. The new estate was to dogs what the prairie used to be to buffaloes. Packs of them came circling, presumably drawn by the stench of my fear. Prince was doing his fruit. Twice the washing line wrapped itself around my legs, bringing me crashing to the dog's level. When I came into view of our house looking like a canine Pied Piper, instead of coming out to help me, my family gathered in the window clutching each other and laughing hysterically.

After the third coat of shampoo, his colours began to emerge. He turned out to be a handsome, intelligent looking dog, black and tan with a white chest. Unfortunately, those classical features only hid his vast reserves of stupidity.

Rubbish skips were his idea of heaven. The first time he indulged this strange hobby, I didn't know what was happening. He began straining at the leash and yelping

8

dementedly. I assumed he was in the grip of a bowel spasm, so I let him off the lead and, without a backward glance, he leapt straight in the skip and began snuffling amongst the rolls of scabby lino and mildewed carpet like an over-zealous truffle hound. Before I reached him, he'd tossed a kid's bike frame over the side, and was hoiking out a rotten dining chair with the same single-mindedness I'd admired in my mum at jumble sales. He lugged that chair all the way home, pausing only occasionally to re-establish his grip and issue a low growl each time I tried to wrestle it from him. We weren't a well-off family, everything we had was second-hand, so I reckon the neighbours thought we'd trained him to bring home anything that might come in handy.

After a while though, it must have become obvious to everyone that we had a very stupid dog. I once took him a long walk up to Baitings Dam where, amongst several thousand square acres of untamed moorland, he managed to find an eleven-foot length of plastic water pipe. Traffic built up behind us as we made our way home, queuing to negotiate the hazard that had become an immovable extension of my idiotic dog's jaws.

Mum's sarcastic crack about getting two dogs came back to haunt her in the July of that year, when my dad arrived home sheepishly cuddling a tiny Golden Labrador. Honey was as cute as a lion cub then, but until the day she died thirteen years later, weighing eight stones and with breath that could kill house plants, she remained convinced she was still a cuddly ball of fluff. When greeting one of us, her whole enormous backside would sway in counter time to her tail, whilst at the other end she'd be attempting to nuzzle the object of her affections, unaware that her hellish breath made her as cuddlesome as a month-old corpse.

Prince and Honey were like Jack Spratt and his wife. They were fed at the same time with the same meal, he from a bucket, she from an old saucepan both placed on a rubber mat in the kitchen. She'd dive into that saucepan grunting and snuffling like a Tamworth pig. Within seconds her pan would be off the mat and we'd hear the metallic scraping and clanging as she bounced off skirting boards and doors, blindly skating it over the tiled kitchen floor. Prince set about his food in a civilised manner, pausing occasionally to lap some water before returning to his leisurely meal. The moment she'd licked her own pan spotless, Honey would take up position behind Prince and for a brief half minute or so she appeared alert and intelligent as opposed to over-fed and indolent. As soon as he lifted his head to lick a stray splash of gravy from his whiskers, she'd be in for a spot more noisy mobile guzzling.

In September that year, we had a family holiday, staying at a rented cottage in Fife. We hired a Volkswagen Camper for the week so conditions weren't too crowded. It all started deceptively well, bowling up the A1 with my dad bellowing out, 'Ohhh, the River Clyde's a wonderful sight...' When we arrived at our cottage, Mum was thrilled with mod cons like the washing machine and fridge. Even us kids stopped squabbling for long enough to ring our mates back in Smallbridge on the upstairs telephone extension.

It wasn't until the first day proper that things began to go badly. We went over to Methyl to do a bit of bathing, relying on the nearby steelworks to guarantee a fairly uncrowded beach. If there was one thing that Prince loved more than skips, it was water. The whole of the North Sea to go at sent him into a frenzy. He could hardly contain himself, bounding over the seats of the caravanette and throwing me off balance as I clambered into a sickly pair of olive green towelling trunks that my mum had ordered through the catalogue. I hated them, but all Mum said was: 'Don't be so bloody stupid. Who do you think you are? Beau bloody Brummell? Do you really think the rest of the world pays a second glance to some puny sixteen year old? They're a perfectly good pair of trunks. Get them on.' I didn't know who Beau Brummell was, but I was willing to bet his mum didn't make him wear trunks that went all baggy the minute they got wet.

The reason I'm telling you about them now is because of what happened the moment I slid back the door of the caravanette. In the distance I'd seen a very attractive girl heading towards us, so I reckoned that if I got my finger out, me and Prince could be down on the beach before she got close enough to get an eyeful of the shameful trunks.

As soon as I opened that door, Prince leapt out and flattened a poor old lady who'd been walking along licking her ice-cream. Then, adding insult to injury and displaying a devastating lack of remorse, he wolfed down her dropped cornet.

My dad went barmy. 'You brainless bugger,' he yelled at me whilst helping the old woman to her feet. I could tell by her expression that the old woman thought Dad was having a go at *her*. Her physical discomfort gave way to brief panic but she stayed quiet, presumably hoping that the bearded madman was part of the same Alsatian nightmare and that she'd soon wake up. But it got worse. 'You're a feckless, lame-brained little closet. What are you?' he continued, brushing sand from the woman's shoulder blades, oblivious to everything but his own anger. The attractive girl rushed up. 'Are you alright, gran?' she enquired, whilst simultaneously throwing me a filthy look and sneering at my trunks.

On the fourth evening, it was Honey's turn for the doghouse. The younger kids were in bed, both dogs lay curled in front of the gas fire, me, our Shelagh and my mum and dad all sat watching Colditz on the colour telly. Whenever Prince was sleeping or relaxing, his bottom lip moved like a pipe smoker's and made much the same kind of subdued plopping noise. If you were stuck in the same room as him for any time, it became as irritating as a dripping tap.

My dad had an ingrowing toe-nail then, so he wore open-toed sandals most of the time. Whenever Prince's lip became too much, he'd stamp a sandalled foot on the floor, whereupon the spectacular clash of buckles would wake Prince and give us all a ten-minute respite. That evening, the plopping was even louder than usual but, when Dad brought down his sandal, Honey woke with a snarling start and bit his bad toe. There was some painful swearing, which was a bit ungrateful considering she'd got shut of his ingrowing toenail.

Next day we went up to Loch Ness where Prince had one of the best matched fights of his life with a huge black Labrador. It was nasty, dog fur and saliva everywhere. My dad and the Labrador's owner were doing their inadequate human best to bring that disturbance of the Highland peace to an end. Our Kathryn, the nine-year-old, knew exactly what to do: after all, she'd had *The Ladybird Book of Dogs* out of the library three times since we'd got Prince. 'Pinch his tenticles, Daddy, pinch his tenticles,' she advised loudly, providing even more amusement for the growing crowd.

Like all good showmen, Prince saved his best trick until last. On the way home, we stopped at a roadside cafe just north of Alnwick. It was about eight o'clock and already growing dark. 'You'd better take silly-guts for a wander,' Mum instructed me, referring, of course, to Prince. That suited me. Two-and-a-half hours cooped in the stressful post-holiday atmosphere of our family caravanette and I was gasping for one of the Number 6 tucked down my socks. I disappeared into the dark whilst the clan trooped into the cafe. At that time, I was new enough to fags for them to send me satisfyingly dizzy, so I maybe wasn't paying as much attention as I should have done to Prince's cavorting. The last I'd known, he'd shot down some dark Northumbrian lane chasing some real or imagined prey. He was forever doing that sort of thing, so I didn't get worried until five minutes had passed and he still hadn't shown.

Eventually there was nothing for it but to go and own up. 'The first holiday we've had in donkeys' years and one way or another, you've managed to ruin it,' yelled my mum, who wasn't above creating a scene in a moderately busy roadside cafe.

We all went out calling for him - no joy. Me and my dad set off in the camper looking for the daft sod, but after an hour we gave up. By ten o'clock they were waiting to close the cafe - so, with the younger kids in tears, it was decided that my dad would ring the police and, with a bit of luck, they'd round him up for us to collect a couple of days later. The cafe proprietor was a kind bloke. He kept telling us that their poodle was always doing the same trick, sometimes disappearing for days. We knew he meant well, but it was different when you were 120 miles from home. My mum and dad were calling Prince from fleabag to shagnasty as we made our way out of that cafe.

It was me who saw him first, silhouetted against the reflected moonlight shining on the Volkswagen. He just sat there, ears pricked, not bothering to run and greet us as he did normally. At first we thought it was because he knew he was in big bother, but it was more the practical problem of bounding about with eleven pounds of dead-weight poodle in his gob that was slowing him down.

My mum went into hysterics. Prince was pulling his usual stunt, snatching his head from side to side, spattering my little brother with blood and defiantly refusing to drop the poodle. The smell of blood and the thought of an extra meal had aroused Honey's dormant instincts, so she'd clamped on to one of the poor poodle's legs.

Eventually I steeled myself and broke their macabre tug-of-war by kicking the dead poodle from between their jaws. My dad went off to tell the unfortunate proprietor what had happened to his dog, but couldn't get any answer. Mum decided to write him a letter and had a lot of trouble getting the wording right. Using a dustpan from the caravanette, my dad dug a shallow grave in the flower bed next to the toilets and buried the poodle.

Prince died five years later, a couple of weeks after a chilly October dip in the Calder. My sister Shelagh got married in the November. At the reception, me and my dad were almost in tears. Put it down to the dry sherry, but I heard myself saying, 'If there's a heaven for dogs, that's where Prince'll be,' and my dad didn't even look nauseated. A bit later on, one of my new brother-in-law's friends began getting belligerent with some bloke I didn't know. When the bride went over to administer her calming feminine influence, my dad called after her; 'Pinch his tenticles, Shelagh, pinch his tenticles.'

May's Harvest

Mary Sara

'*SOMETIMES she felt like the autumn trees - as though all her vitality were seeping earthwards, drawn away from her by irresistible forces. As their leaves turned and faded, fluttered to the ground and were churned in to the mud, so her mood darkened until she thought she would never see the light of cheerfulness again.* Oh, dear,' said May, to the woman in the next bed. 'I don't think I am going to enjoy this one. What have you got this week?'

'An Agatha Christie. And one I haven't read,' was the smug reply.

The selection on the library trolley that was wheeled through the wards twice a week was not large. There were always too many romances, thrillers or westerns to leave much space for anything else. May had always read a great deal and felt very keenly the lack of good reading matter to help the hours and days pass. Thelma was alright in her way, kind and cheerful, but not exactly stimulating company. Still, it could have been worse, she thought. If she had had to have the bed next to the woman who chattered non-stop about 'our Wilfred, our Annie and little Joanie' she didn't think she could have borne it. May turned to her book again. It was that hour between afternoon tea and supper when the ward was hushed. Later would come the bustle of meal serving, eating and clearing. Then the straggling procession of visitors to sit at bedsides, leave untidy bunches of flowers and brown paper bags of fruit and then go again, back to their real lives. May's only visitor wasn't coming tonight because she was going home in the morning - so she had looked forward to a good read instead.

'It's well written but a bit depressing,' she decided. She recognised the feelings the writer was describing well enough, though she reckoned she was now past the autumn and at the winter stage of tree-dom. No vitality left, bare and shivering in the wind and with no spring to look forward to. At this oddly poetic thought, she closed her book and her eyes and let her mind wander.

The trees nearest to Buttershaw Farm had been mostly very old sycamores, shielding the house and barns from the worst of the wet westerlies and snow-laden northerly winds that battered the Pennines for half the year. Their pale spring buds had always cheered her with their promise of milder days when she would be able to leave her chores and go in search of catkins and pussy willow for the old white jug on the kitchen windowsill. Daffodils beneath them starred the struggling spring grass and the shade they gave in summer heat was almost palpable from inside the airless house. The only time she hated them was in late autumn when the leaves fell, mottled with liverish spots like an old person's hands. It was then that she was forced to notice their thrusting, green coated trunks, which made them seem like malevolent beasts threatening the house. Her farmer husband had always said she was 'fanciful' about the trees, plants and flowers he took for granted - and it was not as if she were a 'townee' he would remark. Perhaps she had been. Perhaps they had somehow given her the comfort she needed to cope with the long, isolated days, hard times when sheep prices dropped, the lack of children ... she opened her eyes again.

'Nice snooze?' asked Thelma.

'No, just daydreaming,' she smiled.

That's what Tom had called her sometimes, in the good times. 'Come on Dolly Daydream, I haven't got all day,' when his dinner wasn't on the table when he came in, or she wasn't ready when he was to go down the valley on market day.

She wondered how writers got it all down as they did, in the right order and apparently without leaving anything out. Her memories came to her in such a jumble. Days when she was first married might lead to her widowhood and the selling of the farm or back to her village childhood - all in the same few seconds of thought.

'You'll have to watch her, she's always got her nose in a book, that one,' her father had laughingly said when she was a bride in slippery cream satin, carrying rosebuds.

It was true. She had read everything she could get hold of as soon as she discovered books. Her father would bring her comics and later battered paperbacks from a second hand stall on the market. School and Sunday School had yielded prizes, her mother's employer had passed on dog-eared picture books from her own children and, finally, when she had her first and only job, she could buy and borrow her own.

The remembered thrill of her first public library tickets was as sharp as yesterday. Working as a clerk in the nearest town, she would slip out at lunchtime and return with her allotted allowance - choosing by size to last the week, for want of any better system at first. Later she began to discriminate, tiring of unlikely romances.

For all that, she had fallen for romantic dark looks, strong arms and a man's clear need of her. Funnily enough, he had been a woodsman then and they had courted amongst spinneys and copses below the moors. His knowledge of the trees was deep and she had let him spin words of love round her as he told her of their qualities. Once he became a farmer though, he seemed not to care for them any more, felling for firewood as soon as a tree was past its prime and grumbling about the sycamores being so near to the house.

She did not bother to read the rest of her book. She longed to get back to some of her old favourites at home. Jane Austen was one of her greatest comforts. It seemed that however many times she read and re-read *Pride and Prejudice* or *Emma,* they gave her the same pleasure. The characters were so sharply pinned down by their manners and sayings that she felt she knew them all - and what they would do and sound like outside the novels. Silly Mrs Bennett always reminded her of her aunt who had married a solicitor's clerk and never let May's mother forget that she no longer belonged to the old village or country ways.

'You should have sent May away before she could get involved with someone local,' she would say, in May's hearing. 'Then she would have had the chance to meet someone better placed, gone up in the world, made the most of herself. She was bright enough.'

May had never wanted any other life than the one she knew, returning home on the bus to the cottage which went with her father's job as a shepherd, after work each day and being free to walk the fields and moors she loved, in all

16

weathers. She had always wondered how Jane Austen could have known so much about all kinds of people when she met so few - was so tied and frustrated by duty and convention? It made her think of all her own villagers whose faces and histories were almost as familiar to her as her own.

She could not remember actually ever being told who so and so had been before she married or why Old Joe's leg was crooked or who the end house had belonged to. Like an ever-running stream, the knowledge had always been there, part of the fabric of belonging. Even when she moved up to the isolation of the farm, there were enough callers and visits to the village or market town for the stream to be constantly replenished, at first at least.

'Wuthering Heights would have been a better name than Buttershaw Farm.'

Ashamed of the thought, she checked herself. That was not fair to Tom. They had been happy, at first. It had not been such a doom-laden, bleak place or life. It was not his fault that times became difficult, that his health failed, that they did not have sons to help keep the land he had worked so hard for. With the change in his physical health, though, had come depression and frequent bouts of savage melancholy which deterred casual visitors and gradually left May alone. Her visits down the valley had to be rushed and on the return journey, whenever the farm came into view, she wondered what sort of mood he would be in when she entered the kitchen.

As May remembered her copy of Emily Bronte's classic, she felt again its soft leather cover with spindly gold title on the front and spine, tissue thin paper and tiny print. She remembered too when she had been given it, by Tom, as a birthday-present-cum-peace-offering after he had been particularly withdrawn from her. It meant a great deal to her that he should have gone into the bookshop, in his market stained overalls, smelling of sheep and with his red, weather-roughened hands lifted it down and brought it home for her.

How she had grieved for poor Catherine and Heathcliffe, trembled with Mr Lockwood and felt the winds howl round the gloomy old house. Even now, as she sat up in bed in the comforting warmth of a bright modern hospital, she shivered a little and reached for her bedjacket.

She had made their old stone farmhouse as comfortable and pretty as she could with little money and much ingenuity. In the long winters she had quilted bedcovers, pegged rugs and covered cushions and chairs. Even at his worst times, she knew Tom had been soothed by her quiet busy-ness. The sound of the drawing of thread or rustle of cloth could be heard over the crackle of logs in the hearth or sighing of the wind in the branches outside.

She did not read when he was about. She was lost to him when she read, entering a world where he could not follow. Instead, she read between baking and supper time, washing and dinner time, when she had finished the jobs for the day but he was not yet in.

Since his death and the move back down to the village, she continued to read. Strangely though, once she had unlimited time and freedom, books had lost some of their savour. Her new books now came regularly on a library van that called once a week and she could afford to treat herself to a paperback or two occasionally when she went to town. She bought a few more classics from the same bookshop that Tom had entered to bring her *Wuthering Heights* all those years ago. Gradually her small bookshelves filled.

She thought of them now and looked forward to being home again. A week or so, they had said, but it had been a month. In the over-heated protection of the hospital she was aware that she had missed the subtle changes in the season. From her bed she could see the tops of some dark cypresses, cone-shaped and unbending. Beyond them was a large tree, its upper branches fanning out above the artificial stiffness of the evergreens in a graceful arc. It was an oak, soon to lose the last of its autumn colour and reveal its bare lines. From the way the branches moved and the colour and quality of sunlight that filtered through them, she could guess at the weather, how the air would smell and the wind would feel if she were out there. Now it was disappearing in the dusk as supper was served and the lights came on.

The rush of cool air playing on her face as she walked

slowly to the waiting ambulance next morning lifted her hair and her spirits. Any doubts about how she would manage at home in her weakened state were banished with its promise of freedom. Her cottage was cosy for her return. A fire flamed and sparked in the hearth, her larder was well stocked and a few bronze chrysanthemums stood in a jug on the table. Her neighbours were kind to her.

The first thing she did was to sit in her high-backed wing chair by the bookshelves and take out, one after another, all her favourites. She did not read at first, but placed a small pile on the table for later. She would read this evening, she thought, after she felt rested again. She leant her head back and slept.

She dreamed she was crouching on the stairs, a book on her knees, feverishly but silently turning its pages. If they rustled too much, her mother would realise she had finished the dusting upstairs and call her for some other job. Next she was leaning her elbows on the kitchen table at Buttershaw. Her chin was in her hands, floury apron still on and the scent of sugar, flour and warmth from her baking making a perfumed haven of the low beamed room. The book that lay before her was not a novel - or was it? It described rural life in Gloucestershire in such precise detail and yet with such poetry that May felt she knew the hamlet, the valley and its people as well as she knew her own, though she had never been out of Yorkshire. She was so absorbed that she did not notice Tom enter. If she had, she would have known his mood immediately from the unnecessarily rough way he yanked at the laces and then kicked aside his heavy boots.

'Nothing better to do then? A lady of leisure, are we? 'Salright for some.'

Neither the fresh scones she hurriedly put before him nor the tender way she asked him about his day could dent his self-pitying, angry misery.

May woke suddenly from her doze as if startled by the unshed tears of her dream. Then, to her dismay, real tears began to gather behind her eyelids. They welled and slipped down her cheeks, silently leaving her face wet and soft where they ran. She did not try and check them or wipe them away.

Why was she crying now? It had all been so long ago, and she had forgiven him then and equally readily understood that he was not in control of his moods.

So why now? Was she unwell? She mentally checked her body. No, she was alright. No pain to speak of. Quite rested, in fact. It must have been the book. It had been the beauty of the book. She turned to her shelves.

'Yes,' she crowed, tears dry now and her face beaming. The book had beaten the sadness then, 'Like music is supposed to bring solace,' she thought. 'I didn't have music, I had words.'

The love that suffused the book had given her such joy. The child loved and protected, the family loving and laughing, the wonderful descriptions of the natural beauty around him that the author recalled with such clarity. She had not read it again from that day to this. Indeed, she could not remember if she had even finished it after she had been so crudely brought back to the reality of her life.

And here it was, on the bottom shelf. Just a paperback bought as a treat for herself with some of the egg money. It had the damp, sweet smell of long-closed pages that made her think she should flap it about in the air outside to get rid of the clinging scent like she would get rid of crumbs from a tablecloth. For hours she read, pausing only to make tea, stoke the fire and respond to the solicitous but brief visit of her neighbour.

It was past midnight and her eyes ached when she closed it, reluctantly. She sat in deep thought for many minutes, the only sound being the fire whispering a dying rustle as cooling embers fell through the grate.

The writer had ended the book at his own beginning as a writer - as a child becoming the man and poet he was destined to be. She thought of her own life and its ending, not so far distant now but accommodated contentedly enough.

Rising stiffly from the chair, she went to her bureau and brought back to the table a pad of notepaper and a pencil. She added more coal to the fire, coaxing it back to life. Under the warm glow of the lamp, as the petals of the flowers dropped silently to the cloth, she began to write.

The Swiss Roll Incident

Ian Clayton

IT WAS a Saturday morning like any other really. The main street was filling up with shoppers, people in cars were looking for somewhere to park and it was spitting with rain.

Dawn Jessop skipped up the pavement on her way to buy a jar of jam and some batteries. 'Coowee!' a man shouted from the opposite side of the road. And again, 'Coowee!' - a matey call. It was Parrot Rogers on his way out of the bookies. His bald head shone like a bicycle lamp as he trundled across the street to greet Dawn.

'You want to go steady running across the road like that,' said Dawn, 'you're going to get yourself knocked down.'

'Never mind that, gorgeous, how are you keeping? I haven't seen you for ages.' Parrot gave her a peck on the cheek.

Dawn giggled. She had a lot of time for Parrot, unlike most people round here. They thought he was a bit daft. A lot called him Bungalow because they said he had nothing upstairs. Dawn thought he was more like a big camp frame tent, the sort you'd want to take on your holidays with you. Always cheerful, never under the weather and full of surprises. She called him Parrot because he always wore bright coloured clothes and he never stopped talking.

'Here, I've something for you,' Parrot whispered and reached inside his coat. 'Close your eyes and hold your hand out.' Dawn did as she was told. Parrot placed a packet on her outstretched hand.

'Pudding mix! What the bloody hell...'

'Ssssh, I don't want any bugger knowing. You never know who's watching. Now come a bit closer.'

Parrot reached into his pocket again and produced a Swiss roll marked 'faulty', a packet of dried tomato soup and a 'Chinese style' sweet and sour sauce mix. 'Have these on me, darling, don't say I never give you anything, and don't tell anybody where you got them.' He looked round nervously, hunched his shoulders and grinned.

Dawn placed the contraband into a supermarket carrier

and kissed him on the forehead.

'Oooh! you're a lovely girl,' he squawked, 'you ought to back Sea Pigeon in the three o'clock at Ripon and make yourself a bit of money.'

'Thanks for the tip, but I'm going to have to get off, I've a lot on today.'

Parrot wanted to talk some more, but cantered off down the street picking his nose.

Duggie Andrews sat on a wall outside the amusement arcade. He was watching Parrot. He had been sniffing glue all morning and felt like hitting somebody. Inside the amusement arcade, other youngsters were queuing to play with the Space Invader machines. Duggie swung his heels into the wall, watched them and listened. The machines sounded like sirens and their lights sent flashes into the street. It started to rain a bit faster. Duggie ignored it.

Parrot got back to the council house he shared with his mother just as it started to thunder. He decided to spend the afternoon in front of the telly, but first he made himself a fishcake and poured curry sauce mix on to it.

You'd have to say that Parrot Rogers was seedy. His best coat had emulsion paint on the shoulder. He had once brushed past a painter in the entrance to a working man's club and partly rubbed out a sign saying WET PAINT. He had nicotine stains on most of his fingers because he sucked his Park Drive cigarettes until the red end almost burned his lips. His brown big toe nails poked through the holes in his woollen socks and most of his vests had beetroot stains down the front. One of his favourite pastimes was eating beetroot sandwiches in bed while watching French sex films. He couldn't speak French and he couldn't read the subtitles very well, but it excited him when he saw small blonde women prancing through the woods and swinging their legs on tree branches with their skirts off.

Outside in the rain, Duggie Andrews sniffed some more glue and mixed it with a cocktail of lighter fuel. Dawn Jessop hurried back to her flat, put a load of washing into the machine and sat watching the water run down her window.

Parrot watched the wrestling and decided to have an

hour in bed. He'd been on nights all week at the cake factory and wanted to have his wits about him for the bingo later on at the club. He climbed into bed, lit up a fag and drifted off to sleep. The Park Drive dropped between his mattress and the wall. The sheets smouldered steadily as Parrot dreamed of Templegate tickets, cheese and beetroot. Small flames licked his feet as he dreamed of fireside toast like his mother always made. Spit began to dribble from the corner of his mouth.

'Wake up, you silly bugger!' Parrot's mother called, patting the bedclothes with a damp tea towel, 'You've set the sodding bed on fire.'

Parrot grinned like a big sliced melon.

'It's not bloody funny. You could have burned yourself to death.'

Parrot wasn't too worried. He was always having accidents like that - only last week he'd cut his finger when he tried to see how sharp his razor was.

He sighed, put his feet on the lino and studied his socks. He puzzled his mind trying to work out why the big toe still peeped through even if he put the left sock on his right foot. He didn't puzzle too long, he wasn't a puzzling type of person.

Duggie Andrews was wet through to his feet now. It wasn't that he was too daft to get in out of the rain, but his mind was a whirlpool. The neighbours often said he didn't know whether he was on this earth or Fullers and today was one of those days when he didn't.

Parrot coughed for five minutes on the side of his bed, scratted his balls with his brown nails and stumbled into the kitchen. He moved the unwashed pots over to one side of the sink and had a piss. After his piss, he fried an egg with black bits on, and squeezed it between two slices of white bread from the supermarket. He sat down to eat his tea, picked up the paper at the racing page and tried to count up his winnings. After his sandwich, Parrot decided to trim his nails by biting them.

'You want to stop biting your nails and swallowing them,' his mother shouted from her perch in the corner, 'you'll end up puncturing your lungs.'

Dawn Jessop was listening to some soothing jazz music, stroking her cat and writing her name on the misted window.

Parrot lit up another cigarette, and by mistake tried to light his pencil. The rain showed no sign of abating as Parrot trotted down the main street like a puffed old racehorse. He played at bingo, joined in when the turn sang 'I will survive' and supped a fair few pints. Before time was called, he decided to leave for home. He had read in the paper that the television was showing 'a daring sex comedy made in 1971' and he thought there was a good chance that 'There might,' as he had said to the doorman at the club, 'be a bit of tit in it.'

He hurried down the street, but had to stop for a piss against a wall. The pee coursed into the gutter with the rain. It was chucking it down now. He felt a rough hand on his shoulder. Duggie Andrews swung him round and pinned him against the wall. 'Giz some drugs!' grunted Duggie.

'I don't know owt about drugs.'

'You're a fucking liar - I saw you give some to that punk bird this morning.' Parrot felt a terrible pain as Duggie brought a knee up between his legs. 'Stop pissing me about.'

'I... I... I haven't got any.'

Duggie headbutted Parrot straight in the face and a crimson moon shone down his chops. Parrot threw up on to Duggie's sodden jumper. 'Bastard! You'll pay for that!' He threw Parrot into the rain and booted him in the ribs. Parrot's ribs cracked and the air gushed out of his body. Duggie booted him again and again and then stamped on his ear. He rummaged through his coat pockets, swiss rolls and batter mix fell on to the pavement. Duggie jumped up to run away, but gave Parrot one more kick in his eye for good measure.

Dawn Jessop heard the screams for help and looked from her flat window to see Parrot writhing in agony on the ground. She phoned for the police. The police car arrived and a copper got out and walked over to Parrot's crumpled body. He picked up a Swiss roll and held it like a torch while he looked at Parrot's broken teeth. In the distance an ambulance siren wailed and lights flashed like an amusement arcade. Batter mix washed into the gutter with the rain. It was a Saturday night like any other round here.

The Holy Colonial

Lesley Atkinson

IT is hot, even at seven o'clock in the morning. The heat
hasn't died down from the day before. The air is thick and
smells dusty. This is the summer of 1947 and the snow
which lay on the pavements until late April seems like a
dream now. A gentle roll releases me from the damp sheet.
I fall in slow motion on to the rag rug.

From this upside-down position, I view my sister. She
is deeply asleep. One arm dangles over the edge of the bed
and her fingers are only inches away from the white
chamber pot. I uncurl myself and lie face down on the rug,
breathing in its dusty fragrance. It is so hot! Moving is a
penance, fresh droplets of sweat break out on my top lip.

Standing up, I stagger across the patterned linoleum.
My feet stick moistly to the warm surface, they make soft
sighing noises with each step that I take. One frog-like leap
takes me over to the window. I lean my elbows on the sill
and stare out at the greasy sky.

The tree in the garden is near enough for me to touch.
Not the smallest wisp of air stirs its branches. The tree, like
the morning, is holding its breath. My sister Pat sighs and
moans as she turns over in her sleep.

I tip-toe over to the wardrobe and take out a clean dress
and a pair of cotton knickers. Grabbing my sandals, I run
stark naked into the bathroom. The cold tap runs warm. I
wait, cupping my hands, letting the warm water play over
my fingers. No cool wash to revive me, so I splash the lukewarm water on to all the smelly bits. A swift rub with the
towel and then the struggle to get the tired cotton pulled
over damp limbs. Ugh, it's so horribly hot. I push my wet
feet into the sandals without undoing them.

'Les... Les, is that you?'

My mother's voice floats up the stairs. She mutters
something to herself and walks back into the kitchen.

I shut my eyes tightly, squeezing out all the light until
my eye sockets hurt. I am blind. I have no conscious

memory of sight, but my mind's eye is filled with glowing impressions of shapes and colours. At the top of the stairs now, hands flapping wildly, feet shuffling cautiously, feeling for the top stair. Right hand closes over the round bannister rail, left foot anchored, right foot trembling, poised sickeningly over space.

'What the hell do you think you're doing?' My eyes snap open and my mother's angry face swims up at me. 'You'll break your bloody neck one of these days, you'll kill yourself. Well, you'll get no sympathy from me! Silly bloody games. Who are you meant to be this time? Helen Keller? For God's sake! Get downstairs and get your breakfast. I want you to run a message into Richmond for me. You can take this list to the Holy Colonial store.'

She means 'The Home And Colonial.' Holy Colonial was the best that I could do, aged five. It had become a family joke.

She has burned the toast again. I can hear her scraping frantically. The kitchen smells of bleach and cigarettes.

'Pat awake yet?' My mouth is full of scraped toast, so I shake my head in answer. 'Don't *you* start! It's bad enough having to work in this heat without you sulking all over the place. What are you sulking about anyway? Did you hear, milady?'

'Yes, mum! I'm not sulking...I'm hot! Pat is still asleep...I think.'

She sighs and sinks down on a chair. 'I'm sorry, love, it's this weather. By 'eck, it's so hot!. Look, here's the list and the purse. You won't go off into one of your trances, will you, duck?'

Her tone is brisker now and she holds out a string bag and reads out the list. I nod emphatically, to assure her that I am not only listening but have heard! 'Mum, can't I get this lot from the NAAFI? It's much nearer.'

'No, you can't! I've run a big bill up with them and I can't afford to settle it until the weekend. Don't bloody dawdle neither, we want the corned beef for dinner, not for supper.'

I set off walking backwards, counting the steps which take me away from the circle of houses that make up Cutts

Road. Our house has its blind look on. I have the crazy notion that the houses are sweating. My day-dreaming is interrupted when I trip over the low wall which separates Mrs Tiggar's garden from ours. I tumble backwards and land across one of her flower beds. All the air is knocked out of my lungs, but apart from that I'm alright. I am thinking about getting up when the front door opens and Mrs Tiggar stands there, wiping her hands on her apron. Her horn-rimmed glasses are half way down her nose. There is a cigarette dangling from one corner of her mouth. She grins at me. 'This a social call, Les? You dead or just paralysed?'

'I'm alright, Mrs Tiggar. I wasn't looking where I was going.'

'You daft little devil! You were walking backwards. I saw you! You'll have to pack in this day-dreaming, lass. You'll 'ave a nasty accident one day. You going on a message for your mum?' I scramble up and nod. She gives her red hands a final wipe and presses a half-crown into my hand.

'Get me twenty Woodbines, cock. Have an ice cream out of the change.' She twitches her cigarette end at me and smiles. She can move a cigarette from one side of her mouth to the other, without missing a word. Fascinating!

Even in the shady wood, it's sticky hot. I rest my arms around the broad trunk of a copper beech. Through half-closed eyes I can see hundreds of reddish-brown ants scurrying about in and out of the deep fissures in the hard cracked bark. The wood under my cheek is warm and scented. I can feel every pulse in my body echoing my heart beat. The cracks in the bark look like massive gullies.

There is no more time to rest. Down Saddle Dip, past the other beech trees. Through the briar tunnel where the large white dog roses weep petals. Up the humpty-dumpty hill, to finally squeeze through a hole in the maythorn thicket, which leads out on to the main pavement.

I hold my nose as I pass the public lavatory. In the doorway of the store, Mr Rodger's old boxer dog Viking is suffering. I swat away the flies which are buzzing round his head. He wriggles his eyebrows and pants joyfully at me.

There are skeins of saliva hanging from his jowls and his large blood-shot eyes roll in his head as he twitches his stubby tail.

As I enter the shop, it seems unnaturally dark. Mr Rodgers has two electric fans whirring away. There are the usual delicious smells wafting about, like smoked bacon, tea, cheeses and freshly ground coffee.

My eyes are accustomed to the gloom now and I can see that Mr Rodgers is weighing up sugar into airforce blue sugar bags. The bags stand stiff and straight like airmen on parade. The sugar is carefully weighed and tipped into the bags, then Mr Rodgers' skilful fingers bend, fold and tuck in the tops of the bags. He smiles as he takes the list and the string bag from me. 'Hot today, love. Wait a minute.' He opens one side of the ice cream box. The lid is black and reminds me of the ice box on the Stop Me And Buy One bike. He lifts out a round of creamy ice cream and deftly removes the paper without touching it with his fingers. He places it in a cornet and hands it to me. He nods and smiles as I thank him and slip out of the store. I tip some of the fast melting ice cream into old Viking's dish, then head across the road to a bench. The ice cream is heavenly. I lick my messy fingers and bend down to pick up a stick. The dust is laying thick on the road. If I'm patient, I will be able to draw pictures and sculpture dust cities.

I've just begun to pinch and drag the dust into piles, when two women come walking slowly towards me. One is plump, with grey hair. She is wearing a silky sort of dress, which shines in the sun. Her fat dimpled arms look stran-gled in the tight short sleeves. She isn't wearing stockings and her white buck-skin sandals are so tight, the flesh stands up in the gaps like pink marshmallows. She pulls a limp handkerchief out of her dress pocket and wipes away the sweat from the fat rolls around her neck.

'I shall 'ave to sit down, Doris. Whew! I shan't make it up the slope wi'out a short breather.'

They sit on the bench and ignore me. They assume that I'm engrossed in my dust games. I sneak a look at the other woman. She is a lot younger and very pretty. She looks cool in a white linen dress. Her reddish-gold hair is done like Veronica Lake's, the film star. It's called the peek-a-boo style. Her long legs are encased in sheer nylon and her wedge-heeled sandals are made of crocodile skin. She has a matching bag which she holds in her manicured hands. The older woman stares at her.

'Well, Dotty, 'ave you thought yet, about what you're going to do, when your Stan comes 'ome on leave? I mean, it's all very well saying that folks can gossip an' you don't care! Our Shirley's going on seven now and she's not daft! There is a limit to what she'll swallow. I mean, well, as long as Stan don't find out!'

'Aye, well, so you keep saying, Madge.' She giggles softly. 'I can't think what you're worrying about. You get your fair share of the goodies. Funny, that! *My* Stan. I mean I allus think of 'im as *your* Stan, 'im being your brother. I've almost forgotten what 'e looks like. Eh, it's cruel what this war's done to married couples.'

Madge looks hot and grumpy. Her lips are moving in a sulky way. 'Bloody war's been over this twelve month. Not everyone 'as seen fit to get theirself a Canadian boyfriend. Not that I'll tell Stan. May God strike me dead if I tell a lie. But there are those who would split on yer, before 'e even got 'is boot over threshold and what will you do then?' Madge and I are watching Doris intently.

'I dunno! I just don't know. I'll cross that bridge when I come to it. But I'll say this, Madge. You won't get yer extras if I give up my nice little carry on. There's no denying that! Is there?' Their eyes are locked. Madge has munched her mouth into a thin straight line. Doris is smiling and swinging her curtain of hair gently about her face. Suddenly they both look at me. Do they know that I'm a listener?

Madge puts me out of my misery. 'Eh, look at 'er. 'Ow do they do it? She must be double-jointed, 'er knees is up round 'er ear'oles. Bin crouched down there for ages, 'appy as Larry, bless 'er. I don't think she's seen us, let alone 'eard us!'

Doris gives out with her chiming laugh again. 'Bloody good job an' all. Think what she could pass on if she *'ad* bin listening.' They smile down at my bent back. 'Bless 'er. Come on Madge, I'm melting.' Their voices die away and Mr Rodgers calls to me that the order is ready.

Just in the nick of time, I remember Mrs Tiggar's Woodbines. I buy an ice cream out of the change and drag my hot and tired body home. As I turn into Cutts Road, I can see mum and Mrs Tiggar chatting away nineteen to the dozen, whatever that means!

Mum pauses. She sees me. 'Ere she comes, dizzy Lizzy. Eh, look at the state of her, that bloody corned beef won't be fit to be seen!'

I'm dying from sunstroke and all she cares about is her shopping! I give the Woodbines to Mrs Tiggar, smile bravely and drag my exhausted frame up the path. Water, water, I must have water! I can feel their eyes boring into my back.

'Sarah Bernhardt's got nowt on our Les when it comes to acting.'

Cow! She is an ungrateful cow. They both are!

Pat is curled up in a chair, reading. As I rush to the sink and gulp down cup after cup of beautiful lukewarm water, she looks disdainfully over her specs.

'Lesley, you look terrible. Can't you ever stay tidy? You look as if you've been pulled through a hedge backwards!' I ignore her. I'm wondering if Madge will tell their Stan about Dot's Canadian boy friend.

I decide that Pat is a bitch and that I hate her! I hate my brother Terry too, I'm not keen on mum either. They are all a set of...Here, I go to my private store of all the dirtiest words at my command. I always do this. It's a wonderful release and no-one, but no-one, can do you for it. Let it bloody storm. Roll on thunder and lightning! Roll on bedtime! Roll on tomorrow!

Doing What You Can

Charles Easingwood

'JUST look at yourself, sat there with a half. That's not right, is it? A man's entitled to his pint. And think of the kids: you'd be able to give them a decent Christmas.'

'I know, but what if we get caught? It'll probably mean prison.'

'Don't talk daft - it's just a bit of poaching.'

'It's still stealing though, isn't it? I mean, it's big business now, the trout fishing.'

'Aye, big business for them that's got plenty. We're just doing a bit of business ourselves. Why shouldn't we have a share?'

'Yes, but ...'

'No buts, you're either in or out.'

'Well, the electric's overdue and they're threatening to cut us off.'

'I knew you'd see sense in the end. Come on, this place is getting too crowded. We don't want everyone to know our business, do we?'

Jim led the way to his beaten-up old van. He was determined not to lose it. It was the one thing he had left.

'Right, first off we'll get some detonators and jelly from the quarry.'

'You never said anything about using explosives. I thought we were just catching some fish to put a few bob in our pockets, not blow the buggers up!'

'It's the way to do it nowadays, the explosion stuns or kills the fish and they float on the top. Then all we do is net them, easy.'

'I'm not sure about this. Anyway, the stuff at the quarry's kept in a safe room. Well, you should know, you used to work there.'

'I did, and guess who got the keys cut?' Jim dangled them in front of Dave's face.

'Yeah, but they keep records, don't they?'

'It'll be months before they find out. Nobody works

there any more, remember? Same as everywhere around here. They've taken what they can and cleared off, leaving us mugs with no jobs and no hope of any!'

While Dave thought about that one, Jim wound the window down and lit up a cig. 'You know Frank?' said Jim exhaling out of the window.

'The waggon driver?'

'Yes, that's him. Well, he reckons he can sell as many fish as we can catch. He knows someone in a big hotel in London that'll take all he can get, no questions. That's why we've got to do it on a Sunday night - he delivers down there every Monday. There's no point in just nicking a few fish, we might as well be hung for a sheep as a lamb, mightn't we? I mean, it's not the number of fish we take, is it? If we took one, we'd still be in the same boat.'

'Is that supposed to make me laugh - in the same boat? More like we'd be up the creek without a paddle!'

'What? Oh no, I didn't mean it to be funny, but now you've pointed it out ...' they both chuckled, relieving some of the tension that had been building up.

'Right,' said Jim, 'what about Friday for the quarry?'

'This Friday? Don't you think we should think about it a bit before we do it? I mean ...'

'No! Look, Dave, if we're going to do this then the sooner the better. The more you think about it, the more excuses you'll think of.'

'But shouldn't we plan it through? I know you worked at the quarry but you only drove the dumper truck. I mean, you never had anything to do with the explosives, did you?

'Well, I never actually used the explosives but I watched Joe plenty of times and he explained what he was doing. It's simple. It's easier than you'd think. All you've got to do is connect the detonator to the stick with a length of wire and send a few volts down it - BOOM - it'll be raining fish!'

'Well, if you're sure you know what you're doing...'

'Don't worry. Have I ever let you down before?'

'As a matter of fact you have, umpteen times. Look at that time we were going into the second-hand business.'

'Alright, but don't worry. I know what I'm doing.'

They arranged to meet at Jim's house on the Friday. Dave would say they were playing cards so Jill wouldn't expect him back till late.

'It's bloody amazing! That's what I say. No money coming in and you're off to a card school!'

'It's only a friendly game, love. Just me, Jim and a couple of lads from the old firm. It's more a bit of a reunion than a card school.'

'I bet there'll be plenty of booze knocking about,' began Jill, scathingly, 'you know what you're like when you've had a drink. You think every hand you get is a winner.'

'We're all on the dole now, love. We'll only be playing for pennies.'

'You'd better be, David, or I'll have something to say!'

Dave sighed softly as he pulled up his collar. He felt like a criminal already as he slunk down the backs to Jim's house. He was sure Jill could tell when he was lying. He'd never been able to lie to her. Still, as long as Jim had the story straight, he should be alright.

It was way too early when Dave arrived to set off so they did actually play cards for a few hours, just for pennies. 'At least I'll be able to tell Jill that much with a straight face,' thought Dave.

'C'mon, Dave, it's your deal,' Jim nudged his arm. 'I've told you, don't worry. Just think - this time next week we'll have a few hundred quid to play cards with, not a few hundred pence!'

'I'm alright, just a bit nervous. Once we get started, I'll be okay.'

'I know you wouldn't let me down, Dave. Another half hour and we'll be off.'

They parked the van in the deserted brickworks that had once been the largest employer in the area. Jim thought bitterly that there was still plenty of clay in the quarry but since the housing slump there was no call for bricks, so the company had simply moved on. The union had explained to the men that it was purely for financial gain that the company was closing the yard down. It could have hung on, ridden out the slump as had happened in the past, but no, money and profits meant more than jobs and people. That was one of the reasons Jim felt no compunction about stealing. Everyone seemed to look after number one these days, why shouldn't he?

The quarry was half a mile from the brickworks. The safe room was the last building and they had to cross an exposed area to get to it. The moon was out and Dave was convinced that they could be seen from miles away.

'Don't worry. No-one'll see us. Who's going to be looking at this time of night?' answered Jim in response to Dave's whispered fears.

Once in the shadow of the windowless safe room, Dave felt more at ease. Jim fumbled with the keys.

'I don't know which key it is, I just got the whole bunch copied. I borrowed them one weekend after Joe had gone home. I had to come in at half past six on the Monday to make sure I was first in. Christ! That surprised a few people, me being in early! I remember Joe asking if I'd shit the bed! They took the piss out of me that day, I can tell you. I had to tell them I'd set the clock wrong.'

'Never mind that. Just open the frigging door before someone comes!'

'Well, hold the bloody torch still then! If you'd stop looking over your shoulder all the time, I mean, it does help if I can see what I'm doing!'

Jim managed to open the door and they went in. 'The stuff's kept in airtight boxes, stainless steel they are. Here, give us a hand.' The ammunition style box glinted coldly in the light of the torch as they lifted it on to the table. Jim snapped back the catches.

'Magic. I told you there was nothing to it, didn't I?'

'Just get what we need and let's get out of here!'

Jim was in buoyant mood as they drove home, punching Dave on the shoulder. 'It'll be the same on Sunday, no problem, you'll see.'

'Jill wasn't very happy about me coming out again so soon. I think she thinks we've got a couple of women.'

'She'll be okay once you give her some cash. That's what really gets to people, you know. I'm sure most arguments start over money. I bet she mentioned it again, didn't she?'

'She did. She can't understand how I can afford it. I told her that you and the others paid for a few cans. I think she believed that we weren't playing for serious stakes. She looked through my pockets, you know.'

'All women are like that. Always think you're up to no good. That's why I never got married, I couldn't stand all those questions. *Where've you been? Who with?'*

They played cards and watched TV until it was late enough to set out.

'I've parked the van over on the waste ground again, no need to let the neighbours hear us,' said Jim as he shrugged his coat on. 'Come on, let's get off then!'

Dave remained silent on the journey, his face a grey mask, hiding the turmoil that was going on inside him.

'Alright are you, Dave?' queried Jim. 'You haven't said a word since we set off.'

'Just nervous like. You know I'm not right keen on this thing. I'm only doing it for the kids.'

'Don't fret yourself, man. It'll be easy, you'll see, and then you'll be able to get your lass off your back, pay the bills and still have enough for a few pints.'

'I know all that but it still doesn't make it right, does it? We're still breaking the law.' Dave wasn't expecting much of a response from Jim, he was merely trying to reassure himself that what he was doing wasn't really wrong.

'We might be breaking the law, but don't forget who made them. The people who benefit from them, right? Anyway, we're only following an older law, the law of the jungle!' Jim grinned at Dave as if this platitude relieved them of any blame.

'Right, it's up here,' said Jim as he swung the van onto a rough dirt track. A few minutes later they stopped. 'This is as near as we can get the van, the river's just through those trees.' Jim gestured with his head. 'So let's get those waders on and get cracking.'

'Why are we taking the net first?' asked Dave.

'Well, what we're going to do is rig the net up across the river, downstream from where we blow up the fish, right?'

'Yeah, but can't we just catch the fish in the net like that anyway without blowing them up?'

'I don't know. I suppose we could, but it might take forever. Anyway, if we had a net that big ,we'd never be able to manhandle it. This is just a surface net. It's not very wide, but it's long, so we can sweep the surface of the river. That's why the fish have to be floating on the top so that we can just skim them off.'

Dave left it at that. At least Jim seemed to know what he was doing for a change. They stretched the net as tightly as they could between two trees, half in and half out of the water, the bottom weighted to take it under.

'Right, you stop here and watch for any sign of life. I'll go and blow the fish up.' Jim turned to go.

'Are you sure you know how to do it? What do I do if I see something? What am I looking for anyway?'

'All you've got to do is watch the road.' Jim pointed. 'See there? The Manor's that way so any cars will have to come from that direction. So all you've got to do is watch there when you hear the bang. We'll give it five minutes to see if anyone's heard anything, then it's frying tonight!'

Dave grimaced at Jim's attempted humour. He wasn't in a laughing mood. 'You're coming back here after you've set the stuff off?'

'Yes! I'll set it off and come back here. If anybody comes, we'll be off like a shot, straight down that track there, look.' Jim pointed again. 'That takes us onto the main road. We can go all the way round and get home from the other side, okay? Just give me two minutes then it'll be BOOM!' Dave winced as Jim strode off, looking round to see if Jim's shout had been heard. All seemed quiet.

Dave kept looking round furtively. He felt as though someone was watching him. He muttered to himself under his breath, jumping at imagined sounds.

'Christ! Why's it taking him so long? He could've blown up the bridge on the River Kwai by now! If he doesn't hurry up, I'm going to look for him. Bloody hell, what's he playing at?' Dave twisted his watch into the moonlight. Only two or three minutes had elapsed since Jim disappeared through the trees.

'Shit! I thought he'd been gone ages. This waiting is killing me. Come on, Jim, for God's sake!' Dave tried to keep his eyes on the stretch of road he was watching but he found himself straining so hard that he kept losing focus.

'Jesus Christ! They'll have heard that in Leeds!' Dave groaned as an almighty roar echoed through the trees, shortly followed by a shower of water. He wiped his face, turning wildly from the road to the gap in the trees where Jim had vanished.

'Come on! Come on! What the bloody hell are you playing at, Jim?' The sweat on his back turned cold as minutes passed with no sign of pursuit. His eyes kept returning to the gap where Jim should reappear. 'Christ! Don't tell me he's forgotten his own bloody plan!'

Dave couldn't bear to wait, but he forced himself to watch the road for ten minutes, the seconds crawling, before he dared to go look for Jim. None of his shouts had been answered and he felt a cold chill in his spine.

Slowly, with a last long look at the road, he made for the trees. 'Jim?' he called hopefully, 'Jim? Are you there?' The only sounds were the pad of his feet on the ground and the squeak of his waders. The path through the trees seemed longer than before. He could see it stretched in front of him like an unwelcoming tunnel.

'Jim! Jim!' he called as loudly as he dared. He pushed the trailing branches of the last trees aside, the moonlight bright on the quietly flowing river. His eyes locked onto a fish as it caught the light. He watched it drift slowly downstream to where the lifeless form of Jim gently swayed to and fro in the net's cold embrace.

Out of the Mouths

Jack McGillivray

'MY granny's in Australia.'

'Ah... well... my granny's in the graveyard.'

'M-m-m-my grandad had his leg off and swapped it for a tin one.'

'Yes...but my grandad is living with a fancy woman in Barnsley. My mam says I haven't got to tell anyone.'

Frank Womack clenched his teeth on his pipe to stifle a laugh and watched the two little girls move down the aisle and get off the bus, still chattering. He chuckled to himself and rubbed a hand on the bus window, wiping away the condensation. It made no difference, the layers of grime on the outside blotted out any clear view. But after years of making the same short journey from his home to the Club, he knew where he was. The Club was the next stop.

'Hey up, Frank.'

He looked up and groaned to himself. Coming towards him was Cyril-bloody-Tonks, the village bore and local delegate for the British League of Knowalls. Frank murmured a greeting of sorts and the Knowall lowered himself on to the seat, then went straight into his routine, leaning across so that his mouth was only inches from Frank's ear, as if to impart a closely-kept secret. When he spoke, it was in a stage whisper which carried the length of the bus.

'Now, Frank, I've heard that Eddie Jewkes has got the sack from the Pit. They say he went into the manager's office to sort out a problem with his money and when Mr Garland the manager pointed out that Eddie hadn't taken off his cap, do you know what Eddie said? He said he didn't know that Garland was doing haircuts! I mean...! It was only a joke, but one thing led to another and Garland gave him his cards. They'll miss Eddie at the Pit, Frank. He was a regular worker. Every Tuesday, Wednesday and Thursday. Without fail. Regular as clockwork.'

Frank nodded, kept his pipe in his mouth and survived

38

the few minutes until the bus stopped outside the Club. He was glad to get off the bus and escape from the Knowall.

Above the double doors of the Club, the newly-erected sign proclaiming Skelthorpe Club and Institute (Affiliated 1938) also carried an advertisement for Federation Breweries, the Club's new sponsor. Frank looked up at it with pride for he had been partly instrumental in attracting the brewery to the Club and after, the drop in trade during the miners' strike, things were just beginning to return to normal.

He walked into the Club, passed the snooker tables and entered the Big Room. As usual, he was early and the Club was almost deserted. By the time he had covered the twenty yards to the bar, his pint of bitter was waiting for him. He gave his customary greeting to Fred the steward.

'How do, Fred. Good weather for fiddling.'

Fred grinned and gave his stock reply: 'Nay, I wouldn't dare fiddle when there are so many bloody Yehudi Menuhins in this place.'

As he spoke, he reached for a bundle of letters propped on one of the glass shelves behind the bar and passed them to Frank. Slowly, checking each one to see they were all addressed to him - Mr F Womack, Concert Secretary - Frank put them into his coat pocket and picked up his pint. Fred was rubbing the top of the bar with a cloth, quietly humming to himself, waiting until Frank had taken his first long drink of the day before speaking.

'Oh, there's a stranger waiting over there for you, Mr Womack. Says he'd like a word.'

Frank turned his head. A pale faced youth in his late teens, sitting at a table in the centre of the room, looked apprehensively towards him. He walked over to the youth, straddled onto a stool and put his pint on the table top. 'Evening, lad. I'm Frank Womack, Concert Secretary. What can I do for you?'

The young man tried to smile but his nerves showed. Frank took his pipe from his pocket, searched for his matches and waited for him to answer.

'Er, well... I know you're busy and there's probably a proper system... but you see I'm a ventriloquist... er... I'm hoping to become one. I'm on a job training scheme to learn how and I was wondering if I could have an audition. If that's okay with you, Mr Womack?'

Frank managed to light his pipe at the third match. 'I don't know, lad. Auditions are the first Monday in the month and you have to be a registered artiste - for tax and all that.'

Disappointment spread across the boy's already unhappy features. 'Oh,' he said. Slowly his chin lowered to his chest.

Frank cursed himself for being tactless. 'What's your name, lad? Your face looks familiar.'

'Jewkes, Mr Womack, Harry Jewkes, and you might have seen my photo in last week's Chronicle. I won the All-England Junior First Aid Competition. It doesn't help in getting a job though.' Heartened by Frank's interest, Harry Jewkes began to relax and continued: 'Of course, I wouldn't use my real name. I've thought of a stage name. Well, two actually... one for me and one for the dummy. Do you think that Tebbit and Picket would go down well?' He looked across at Frank, waiting hopefully for his approval.

'Aye, it sounds catchy enough. Where's your dummy then? I expect he's Tebbit... eh?'

Harry nodded and his face brightened. From beneath the table he pulled out a black plastic bin-liner, reached a hand inside and slowly lifted out the dummy Tebbit.

The effect on Frank was immediate. He spluttered, coughed and struggled for breath, trying to hold down the laughter that was erupting inside him. Finally he managed to speak. 'Sorry, lad... must have got water in my pipe.'

The dummy Tebbit was a pitifully tatty, homemade travesty of papier mache. Its face, crudely fashioned, was painted with magnolia emulsion and it had lips cruelly daubed in vivid red lipstick. Two table-tennis-ball eyes were fixed lopsidedly and, with an ill-fitting, loose-hanging lower jaw, the dummy had the look of a startled drunk. The body, hideously misshapen, was clad in a torn T-shirt and the legs were mercifully concealed by a pair of girl's pink jeans. The dummy had no feet.

Harry Jewkes held the dummy at arm's length and looked at it, his eyes glistening with pride. 'I made it myself, you know, Mr Womack. Of course, when I get going, I'll have a proper one. Miss Sedgewick at the Job Centre says they'll get one from London for me... if I make a go of it.'

Frank shook his head in disbelief. 'Yes... well, I suppose London is the best place for dummies. Jewkes, you say? Are you related to Eddie Jewkes?'

Harry nodded. "He's my dad but he's been sacked at the Pit. That's why I need to get working straight away. My mam and dad still have to pay off money they borrowed during the strike and Dad says there's no chance of him getting another job. Well, he's forty-one...'

Frank looked thoughtfully at the two of them. It was debatable which was the more miserable looking, but probably the dummy had a slight edge. Glancing at the wall clock, he realised that the quarterly meeting of the trustees committee would start in half an hour. He looked across at Harry and smiled reassuringly.

'Tell you what I can do, Harry. We need a spare barman for the trustees meeting. Eight pounds for two hours and Fred will fix you up with a white coat. And until the next audition night you can be practising. What do you say?'

'Yes, I'd like that. It gives me time to polish my act.'

'It's only a small room with a tiny bar. These trustees think they're a bit posh, you know. It's the doctor, old Patterson the magistrate and Garland the pit manager. But you'll manage fine - it's just serving sandwiches and beer.'

An hour later, the trustees meeting was well under way. Young Harry Jewkes had quietly stocked the bar and had brought plateful after plateful of sandwiches from the Club kitchen. He was not a little awed in the presence of the local dignitaries, but the occasional nod of approval and regular wink from Frank had helped him through the evening.

Eventually, Mr Akroyd, Club president and the nearest thing to royalty in the village, rapped his gavel to close the meeting and signalled it was time for refreshments.

Shoulders jostled shoulders and arms reached over arms as the trustees piled their plates with sandwiches and called out their drink orders.

Ian Garland, manager of Skelthorpe Colliery, a fleshy, hulking six-footer, had downed his third pint in as many minutes and decided he needed a fourth. Beneath his chair, remnants of ham and cheese lay where they had fallen from hastily grabbed sandwiches, littering the highly polished floor. He pushed back his chair, hoisted himself to his feet, turned and yelped in alarm as his legs separated in opposite directions. The soles of his shoes, lubricated with the greasy morsels, scrambled in vain for a foothold as he slipped noisily under the table. He tried to grab the edge of the table but the momentum of his overweight body snatched away his grip and he screamed as his shoulder came out of joint.

The trustees, stunned, halted in mid-bite as Garland's moans drifted from beneath the table. No-one knew what to do. Only the young Harry Jewkes reacted quickly. He vaulted over the bar, unceremoniously pushed the gawping magistrate out of the way and pulled Garland out by his legs.

'Quick, Mr Womack - hold him down!'

Frank knelt down unquestioning and placed his hands on the chalk-faced Garland's chest. Harry took hold of his arm and, with a twisting tug, clicked it noisily back into place.

'Phew! Thank God for that...' said Garland as the colour returned to his face. 'And what's your name, lad?'

'Jewkes. Harry Jewkes. I'm Eddie's son.'

No-one breathed. All eyes were on Garland whose mouth twitched nervously as he tried to smile. 'Oh. Er... me and your dad had a bit of a misunderstanding. Tell him he can start work tomorrow... and if you want a job, you can come too.'

Harry's face showed no emotion as he walked back to the little bar, reached over it, picked up the black plastic bin liner and walked without a word from the room. He closed the door quietly and everyone stared at it in silence. Slowly it opened a few inches and the dummy's head appeared. Its home-made mouth slumped open and it uttered one word.

'Gollocks!'

The door closed and Garland turned to Frank Womack. 'What the hell was that, Frank?'

Frank took a long pleasurable pull on his pipe and blew out the smoke slowly. 'I believe his name is Tebbit, Mr Garland.'

Elsie

Chris Murdoch

ELSIE was wonderful. Everybody said so.

'Isn't she wonderful?' they said and: 'I hope I'm as wonderful when I'm her age'.

Mondays and Thursdays, Alma, the home help, came in to do the rough. There was very little rough to do in Elsie's purpose-built, sheltered housing scheme bungalow, with the pulley over the bath and the bell to push if she felt frightened in the night, so Elsie and Alma ate biscuits instead. Elsie made the biscuits every Wednesday morning, ready for her niece's sons who always came for tea.

Her married niece Marge came on Sundays with her husband Stanley and nearly grown-up children Wayne and Darren. They arrived just after two, pulling up outside the bungalow and unloading Elsie's Sunday dinner from the boot of their Ford Fiesta. Marge said it saved her time and anyway, who wanted to spend Sunday afternoons washing pans? Marge said it was no more trouble to cook for five than for four and all she had to do was to pop Elsie's dinner into the microwave oven, pop the microwave oven into the back of the Ford Fiesta and Elsie could have her roast beef and Yorkshire pudding on the table in front of her before Marge got her coat off.

Then, while Stanley and the boys argued over The Big Match, Elsie and Marge settled down to talk over the week's events. Elsie told Marge all the bits of gossip that Alma had told her on Monday and Thursday and Marge told Elsie nearly all that she and Stanley had been up to that week. Then Marge made a fresh pot of tea while Elsie, saving the best till last, told Marge where she'd been on Saturday with Dot.

Dot was Elsie's unmarried niece and Elsie said that just because Dot had chosen not to have a husband and two great lads to chase after, that didn't mean that she had to move in with Elsie and look after her instead. So Dot lived in a flat and took her auntie out for days and all her friends agreed that Elsie certainly was wonderful.

Every Saturday morning, Dot called for Elsie in her Peugeot GTi and off they went. They visited new and modern shopping centres at the end of motorways and towns with Roman walls. They ate pub lunches in country inns and tried out restaurants from the guide books Dot kept underneath the dashboard of her car. They avoided stately homes because Elsie said that was where old people went on days out.

On Wednesdays, Marge and Stanley went to Asda after work. Marge said that Wednesdays were nothing like as busy as weekends and anyway, with late night shopping and a fridge-freezer, it didn't matter when you went.

When their parents went shopping, Wayne and Darren caught the bus outside their school and crossed town to go to Elsie's for tea. Elsie made them syrup sponge and baked apples stuffed with currants and jam roly-poly and didn't insist that they finish their main course first. Sometimes she didn't bother making a main course at all and the three of them had two puddings instead. Then she got down the jar of pennies that she kept behind the non-stick pans that Marge had bought her and she'd never used and got out the tin of biscuits that she'd made that morning and the three of them played gin rummy till Marge and Stanley came to collect their sons. Elsie let the boys keep their winnings and topped up the jar on Thursday morning when Alma collected her pension.

Don't imagine that Alma and the nieces took up all Elsie's time, or that Elsie's weeks were always so regulated. The nickel-plated model of Concorde mounted on its hardwood stand on top of the TV set testified to that.

Alongside the model was a framed photo of Elsie posed against that famous nose, mementoes of her 80th birthday present to herself. Dot had laid on in-flight champagne and organised the air hostesses into singing Happy Birthday mid-Atlantic. Marge had bought the pans.

A year later, Elsie went to Austria. The coach had stopped at the end of her street. Elsie thought that toilets on buses were a good idea and the stewardess was prettier than the ones on Concorde. She gave a talk about it later at the sheltered housing luncheon club and said she'd do it again if her ship came in and this time she'd bring back a husband. Elsie had never had a husband.

The Sunday after Easter, Marge and Stanley brought Elsie's dinner round as usual. A slice from the joint, cabbage, carrots and a roast potato. The boys did not come. This Sunday they were playing football instead of watching it. Elsie's dinner came out hot but unappetizing and somehow Elsie couldn't fancy it. She said the microwave oven took away the smell. So Marge scraped the plate while Stanley heated Elsie a tin of soup. They whispered together in the kitchen. Elsie had never refused her dinner before. Elsie never refused food.

Stanley put the soup on a tray and took it into the sitting room. Elsie wasn't there. Stanley called Marge and together they opened the bedroom door. Elsie was lying on her bed.

'Bring me teeth, Marge, I've left them by the sink.'

'Go on, Stanley,' whispered Marge, 'you go.'

Marge raised Elsie's head on her arm and helped her settle her teeth.

'Thanks, love,' said Elsie, 'I wouldn't like to die without me teeth in.'

Marge said not to talk so daft and that she and Stanley would sit awhile, while Elsie got her head down.

An hour later, with Stanley holding one hand and Marge the other, Elsie died.

Dot had arrived by the time Marge had gathered herself together enough to lay out the body. It was perhaps just as well. If Dot had not seen the evidence with her own eyes, she'd never have believed that Elsie was in fact her uncle.

Later, when the shock had worn off a bit, the sisters agreed that nobody would ever have guessed. And Elsie was indeed wonderful.

The Coat

Simon Bond

EVERYONE met at the benches. The benches were two old wooden seats beside a small expanse of overgrown grass, strewn with litter and dog dirt. It lay just beyond the main road running through the town. Almost any time, day and night, kids from the surrounding housing estate could be found hanging around there.

One bright, cold, Sunday afternoon, Tommy Wilson made his way to the benches to see if anyone was around. He was a thin, dark haired boy of thirteen and, as usual on Sunday afternoons, he was bored. He had waited in most of the day, hoping somebody would call for him but no one had, so he'd come to find them. There was sure to be somebody at the benches. There always was.

Sure enough, he found four of them: Greg Phillips, Dazza Johnson and John Darton. And there was Lenny Pearson. Tommy approached them casually, hands in pockets, trying not to look too eager for company. Lenny Pearson cast a disdainful eye over him.

'Alright,' Tommy said.

The others nodded a greeting.

'What you been doing all day?' enquired John.

'Not much.'

'New coat?' asked Greg.

Tommy nodded, pleased that someone had noticed his new cagoule, a bright blue and red designer coat. It was smart and fashionable. More importantly, he had actually chosen it and paid for it himself. Normally, such things were left to his mother.

'It's alright, isn't it?' Greg said.

'It's smart, isn't it? agreed Dazza.

'I've seen better,' Pearson said. He and Tommy disliked each other. Tommy hoped he would soon be on his way. He did not normally hang around with them. Usually, all they did was sit around the benches and talk. Then, after half an hour, Tommy would be as bored as he had been indoors, but at least here he would be bored along with his mates.

This afternoon however, something else was afoot.

'We're off to the Rovers match,' John informed him.

Tommy just said 'Oh,' and tried to hide his dismay. He didn't care for rugby. Besides, he had never been to a game on his own before. He'd only ever been with his dad.

'Are you coming?' asked John.

'No, I don't think so.'

He felt stupid but he also sensed that Lenny Pearson was behind the idea. Neither Dazza nor Greg were keen on rugby. John was, but he never went out of his way to attend matches.

'Come on,' Greg said, 'there's nothing else to do except sit here bored out of our heads.'

Now that suddenly seemed a fine alternative to Tommy. 'I don't like rugger much,' he said.

'Me neither,' agreed Greg, 'but it's somewhere to go.'

Tommy was losing. 'I haven't got any money,' he protested. Though to be honest, he did have a little.

'We're off to sneak in,' Pearson said, grinning.

Tommy's heart sank and his face said what he thought.

'It's easy,' John assured him, 'everybody does it. There'll only be a couple of coppers about. Come on.'

Not interested in arguing the issue, they made off in the direction of the rugby ground. Tommy reluctantly followed, nursing a sense of foreboding.

He fell in with Greg and Dazza. Greg, who took a keen interest in clothes, asked Tommy about his new coat. Dazza kept quiet - he always kept quiet. He was a funny lad, Dazza.

John and Pearson strode on ahead. Most likely, Pearson hadn't been able to find anybody to go to the match with, so he'd roped John in. John was okay really, but you sometimes got the impression that, given the choice, he'd rather be off with the likes of Lenny Pearson and getting into all sorts of trouble than be hanging around with them. Tommy wished he'd stayed at home.

They could hear shouting from the terraces as they walked past the allotments near the ground. It was ten minutes before kick-off and most people who had tickets for the match were inside already. The ground was a small compact affair located behind a row of terraced houses. A few latecomers still milled round but the immediate vicinity of the ground was quiet. All the better for sneaking in.

Tommy felt a knot of tension in his gut as they approached the ground. He wanted to turn back, but he was scared of what Pearson might say.

Their route took them past one set of turnstiles. Tommy speculated that he probably had enough money to go in but he wasn't keen enough on rugby to pay for the privilege of watching it.

Pearson came to a halt. They stood before the back wall of the ground which ran behind the grandstand. Behind them was an open field. 'If you get a good run up,' Pearson said, gesturing at the open expanse, 'you can get in here.'

'But it's too high!' Tommy exclaimed.

'Not with a good run up,' Pearson said, giving Tommy a withering glare.

'What about the barbed wire?' asked Greg. He now looked less than happy about the whole idea. He was a big, heavy lad who didn't fancy his chances of getting up the wall. His doubt gave Tommy fresh hope. If two of them backed out, well, that wouldn't be so bad.

'It's wide on top,' assured Pearson, 'so once you get up you can either jump over the wire or slide under it. I've done it loads of times.'

Greg looked unconvinced. Even Dazza looked doubtful. And Tommy had visions of ripping his face on the wire going under, or catching his foot jumping over and going head first. John sensed their unease. 'Isn't there anywhere else?' Pearson looked disgusted and moved them on.

They went back the way they had come, past the turnstiles. This time Pearson took them behind the terraces which ran parallel to a row of houses, with only a narrow alleyway between the walls of the ground and the back yards. Dogs yapped at them as they passed. Looking up, they could see people standing on the terraces.

Pearson brought them to a halt mid-way down the alley.

The wall here had no barbed wire but was crowned instead with a spiked metal fence. For all that, the wall, peppered with foot holes, looked easier to scale. The fence above also looked more promising than the barbed wire for its spikes were joined by metal strips just wide enough to put a foot on and leap over.

Above them, the crowd was jeering and shouting. The game had kicked off. It filled the boys with a new sense of urgency. Pearson was agitated, sneering contemptuously at Tommy as though he was responsible for the game kicking off without them to witness it.

'This's higher than the other place,' Greg complained.

'The other was better,' muttered Dazza.

'Well, it's up to you,' said Pearson and again Tommy got the feeling that it was his fault.

Perhaps it was. He began to feel that the others were holding back because of him. Perhaps without him, the others would already be over the wall. He began to feel that he had to get over that wall, for John and Dazza and Greg's sake, at least.

The noise from the terraces suddenly grew.

'Somebody's scored, I bet,' said Dazza.

'Please yourselves,' said Pearson, and began to scale the wall. He got high enough to grab the fence and haul himself up. Then he scrambled up the fence, put a foot on one of the metal strips and went over. He landed heavily at the other side, then he was gone into the crowd.

Tommy hated him! Pearson had only strung them along so that if they were caught, there would be somebody else to share the blame, but in the end he'd grown tired of them. Tommy was glad to be rid of him but the idea of getting into the ground was now fixed in his mind and there was no backing out.

'That looked easy enough,' said John. He was more amiable with Pearson gone but impatient to see the game all the same.

'It's still high,' said Greg.

'I heard about somebody who tried to get over that fence and slipped on the top,' volunteered Dazza.

They looked up at the ominous spikes. A far worse prospect than barbed wire lacerations loomed before them.

'They call him scabbyknackers now,' added Dazza.

'Let's go back to the other place,' Greg said. Nobody argued.

As they hurried down the alley, back to the wall with the barbed wire, the sound of the crowd rose again.

'Sounds like a right match,' said John.

'Come on, come on!' Tommy barked. His heart now beat furiously with the desire to be inside the ground.

'Here then?' asked John impatiently when they reached the spot.

Tommy and Greg exchanged glances. Suddenly Dazza moved back onto the open field and took a run. He jumped and grabbed the top. John rushed forward to push him up. Dazza made it up the wall and carefully slid under the wire. He snagged his trousers but easily freed himself and, though his face passed within inches of the wire, he went through unscathed.

John turned to Tommy and Greg. 'Who's next?' he asked. Neither of them responded. 'Come on, I'll give you a push.'

Tommy was suddenly unnerved by the wire again. 'Can't we look for somewhere else?' he pleaded.

John impatiently pushed him aside and went up. He made the climb easily and perched for a few moments at the top of the wall. Then he jumped over the wire.

'I'll go now,' insisted Tommy, unable to stand the idea of being outside the ground on his own. He ran at the wall and scrambled to the top. He looked around but could not see John anywhere. There were no policemen around or groundsmen about either, so, after a moment's hesitation, he jumped.

He felt a sharp jolt which caused him to swing back into the wall. He heard the sound of tearing and then he was on the ground. His arm smarted with pain and he inspected it. The sleeve of his coat was torn almost in two, snagged on the barbed wire. Through the tear he could see the bare flesh of his arm and a red gash.

He walked around the back of the grandstand and found John and Dazza. Lenny Pearson was nowhere to be seen.

'I've torn my coat,' he said limply.

John looked astonished. 'How did you do that?'

Dazza just stared at the sleeve.

'Caught it on the wire.'

'But it was easy.'

Soon they lost interest in his misfortune and went back to watching the game. Tommy had no interest in it at all. The only thing he could think about was his coat. He kept looking at it. His brand new coat. The one he had saved for and chosen himself. His coat. He wished Greg was there but he'd no idea what had happened to him.

When the home team went over for a try and the lads around him started jumping up and down and singing in delight, Tommy felt no inclination to join them. He hated the crowd, hated the game, and when the hooter sounded for the end of the first half, he walked away without saying a word to anyone. He left through the main gates which had been opened at half time for anyone to walk in free.

As he walked away from the ground and the noise of the crowd, he clutched his arm. He didn't mind the pain. Just the torn coat.

He went back to the benches and sat wondering what he would tell his parents. He couldn't think of a plausible excuse. But neither would they believe that he had torn his new coat trying to sneak in to watch a sport he didn't much like - and especially when he had enough money to pay. They would be furious and he felt his stomach churn in apprehension.

It was almost dark before he went home. It started to drizzle as he walked down his street. He was weeping from frustration and pain and anger. Also out of a sense of loss, and not just of the coat. Though what else he had lost he wasn't really sure.

Green Girdle

Pamela M Pennock

I CHECKED the file again just to be sure: Harper, Eleanor, aged 54, 18 Heatherfield Close, Saltburn by Sea. Yes, it had to be her, everything fitted, except, of course, the cancer.

I was working at the time as personal secretary to Mr Michael Dawson, a consultant surgeon engaged in research into breast cancer, in particular the value of partial mastectomy and radiotherapy as an alternative to the usual radical surgery. I was doing the spadework, inviting patients of twenty years or more ago to a special clinic 'in the interests of research.' Many, I knew, would have died long since, but there would be survivors, often completely unaware that their 'lump' had been deadly malignant.

I wondered into which category Miss Harper would fall. I read her notes with misgivings. 'Enucleation of right medial carcinoma - some involvement of lymph nodes - prognosis poor.' Not much hope. Yet I wondered. The surgery had occurred twenty years ago, one year before I had moved into her form at the High School, yet I could not remember ever seeing her look ill or take leave.

Miss Harper had been senior mistress of lower school, an autocratic mix from the pages of Angela Brazil or *Daisy Pulls It Off*. She was a substantial lady, square of face and body, Edwardian in dress and spirit, imperial, imposing and quite terrifying. Her voice never rose, like that of the snappy little French mistress, but could turn to steel and, like her blue eyes, which missed nothing, uncover secrets and lies with ruthless efficiency.

Her clothes spoke of restraint and discipline: straight ankle-length skirts of plain tweed or worsted, topped with cream high necked, long sleeved blouses, vyella in winter, pure silk in summer. Always, pinned at her breast, was a gold fob watch, which she only had to touch to send young feet scurrying and hearts thumping. Sometimes, I had tried to imagine her as a child, running free in the garden of the great house where she then lived with her elderly mother, or along the stretch of golden sand that was Saltburn. Had there ever been a time when her limbs had been free to rejoice in the sun, wind and sand as mine had done? Had she ever tucked dress into knickers to jump the waves, fished in the rock pools or kissed a boy under the pier? The idea seemed preposterous, yet, occasionally, there was a hint, like when a curl sprang free from the severe cut of her hair, or a smile softened the austerity of her features, of the young, almost pretty girl she had once been.

At low tide, we had played hockey on the beach, marking out the pitch on the damp sand, whilst she perched like a great bird of prey on the cliff top promenade above. With splendid confidence, she had controlled the game with whistle or the movement of an arm, and on the final blast we had formed up in pairs to stagger up the steps and receive her comments:

'A shambles girls, a shambles. Reds missed at least two goals and Blues - you have no idea of team work. Pamela, don't slouch.'

On some days a salt wind would sting our cheeks or sea fret enfold us in its damp shroud, but she would make no concessions. In voluminous cape she had towered, like some great and ancient God, unmoved by either the elements or unruly girls.

In class she had been relentless, driving us on to academic success and purity of thought and mind. I found both difficult and she knew it. I would have been content to have been demoted to a lower form away from constant struggle and her eagle eye, but I wanted a green girdle, the passport to success in upper school.

Green girdles had been awarded for deportment coupled with good behaviour, and those fortunate enough to be entitled to wear one became the school elite: in Brodie terms 'the creme de la creme.' The emerald sash brightened the uniform drab navy tunic and endowed its owner with a special allure and confidence which I had longed to possess. But no matter how I had tried, walking at home with a book on my head and curbing my chattering tongue, Miss Harper had always caught me off guard and dashed my hopes once again.

I had begun to hate her, resenting the power she appeared to have over me and wilfully wishing I could do something to destroy her cold self-sufficiency.

Then one day I had gone too far.

We had been playing hockey on the beach as usual when someone called 'Hey-up, we've lost Boadicea.' Twenty-two pairs of eyes had gazed upwards and, finding the cliff top empty, made the most of the situation. Mousy Rendall had been despatched up the steps to stand sentry and the rest of us gave ourselves up to freedom and thin April sunshine. Some girls had rushed to the edge of the sea, swinging seaweed and tearing off their shoes, but the rest of us had merely laid on the sand or carved pictures in it with the sharp end of mussel shells. Pierced hearts and initials had given way to more vulgar expressions and I had been busily engaged in adding the outline of a watch to an enormous pair of breasts when a shadow had fallen across the sand. Large laced-up leather shoes obliterated my masterpiece and a dreaded voice spoke quietly:

'I shall expect a thousand word essay on Exhibitionism, Pamela, first thing tomorrow morning'.

The funny thing is that I was still drawing breasts almost twenty years later, round circles with a dot in the centre and a cross to indicate the location of the tumour.

My face flamed as I looked once more at the diagram in the file marked 'Harper.' I remembered the crude sketch in the sand, and the indent for a watch, precisely where the cancerous growth had been.

My fingers shook as I typed out her invitation and, whilst I prayed with all my heart that by some miracle she had survived, the thought that I might see her again filled me with shame and trepidation.

She replied, in a firm hand, fountain pen on Basildon Bond, that she would be pleased to attend Mr Dawson's clinic on Wednesday 14th at 2pm. My God, she'd beaten it! The insidious growth that had invaded her immaculate body had been excised so completely that no spoor had survived to contaminate it further. Not for the first time, I wondered how she would look - as I remembered her, or frail and old after a lifetime of hard work and dedication? Would she recognise me? I had signed the letter in my married name. No reason for her to connect P. Pennock with Pamela Hart, the terror of Upper 1.

I dressed carefully on the morning of the clinic. I wanted her to notice how tall and straight I had grown. I had washed my hair the previous evening and brushed it into a neat, shining bob, of which I felt sure she would approve. I polished my shoes, trimmed my nails well below their normal length and applied just a small amount of make-up. Finally, at lunch time, I donned a freshly laundered white hospital coat and handed the files to Mr Dawson.

At precisely two o'clock, cool, efficient and in complete control, I admitted our first patient, Miss Eleanor Harper.

She had changed, there was no doubt about it. She was smaller than I remembered and much thinner and her smooth face was trellised with fine lines. Her hair, still cut in the same severe style, was grey and I knew at once what she would be wearing beneath the long tweed coat which reached almost to the ground.

Her eyes looked into mine, upwards now, for I had grown as she had shrunk, and a wry smile touched her face.

'Now let me see,' she said, drawing off her gloves and pointing a finger in my direction. 'Can it possibly be - Pamela Hart? Nineteen-forty-eight, if I remember correctly.'

'That's right, Miss Harper. It's Pamela Pennock now.'

'Of course. Well now, Pamela, how very nice to see you after all these years - and working hard, I hope?'

'Er - yes thank you, Miss Harper.'

The voice of a child. I could sense Mr Dawson's amusement and flushed with embarrassment. In one short minute, she had stripped away my composure and left me nervous and defenceless.

I showed her to the seat Mr Dawson held ready and sat down a few feet away at my own desk.

He began gently to explain his reasons for wishing to see her and she answered with a quiet dignity. Then they looked across at me, smiled and whispered conspiratorially and I felt vulnerable - an interloper in an adult world.

Mr Dawson stood up.

'I'll leave you now, Miss Harper, just for a few moments, in the capable hands of Mrs Pennock. If you wouldn't mind undressing, I can then make my examination.'

This was my cue to exude warmth and reassure the patient, a role in which I was well practised and confident, but today I remained frozen at my desk.

'Come along, Pamela, take my coat, there's a good girl, and let's get on with it.'

I jumped to my feet and went towards her, tongue-tied as she began to undress, talking as she did so.

'Put my watch on your desk, dear, I don't want to forget it when I leave. That's right, hang up my blouse, we don't want it to crease, do we? Mr Dawson seems to think very highly of you, Pamela. I am very pleased you have done so well for yourself. Now then, are we ready, do you think?'

She sat before me on the upright hospital chair, spine erect, head high. My eyes were drawn to the familiar scar that mutilated her upper body. A purple line ruptured the skin from shoulder to waist, crossed by another where the breast had been, to a point beneath her arm.

Her blue eyes held mine, just as they had before, but for one brief moment I glimpsed apprehension in their depths and her fingers clung tightly to the arms of the chair.

Suddenly, I understood her need. I took a deep breath.

'Yes, quite ready, Miss Harper,' I answered briskly, 'but let me cover your shoulders. We can't allow our patients to catch cold, you know.'

I walked to the inner door and alerted Mr Dawson. He entered and examined, tapping and listening, whilst I took notes - cool, impersonal and dignified.

'Thank you, dear,' said Miss Harper later as I held open the door for her. 'It has been delightful to see you once again and I must say that I am proud of you.' Then, once more, she wagged a finger. 'But you still tend to slouch just a little, Pamela. Such a pity about your green girdle.'

A Rose By Any Other Name

Margery Owen

ROSE'S parents had a fish and chip shop and she hated it.
It seemed to have cast a blight on her life for as long as she
could remember. The eight-year-old comedians in the
school playground intensified her hatred.

'Stinky Rose, watch yer nose!'

Even teachers occasionally made a veiled hint. 'Er, Rose
dear, would you open that window near you? It's a bit hot
in here.' The excuse was added at the sight of Rose's hurt
little face. She knew her clothes always retained that fishy
odour which accompanies all fish shop workers. Her parents
were scrupulously clean, but as the shop adjoined the
house, there was no way to avoid the smell.

When Rose reached the age of thirteen, she was expected
to do her bit in the shop. In the back store room she twirled
the potato peeling machine, kept the vinegar bottles filled
and sorted the newspapers: the clean ones for wrapping the
fish and chips, the doubtful ones for wiping up spilt
dripping. None of your Lancashire cooking oil in this
Yorkshire shop. And all the time, Rose hated it.

Why couldn't her father have been a milk man or a coal
man? Clean or dirty, there was no smell to either occupation.
As she toiled in the back of the shop, she vowed she'd never
marry a man who owned a fish shop - if any man would ask
her to marry him while holding his nose.

Rose didn't marry a fish and chip shop owner. Fred
worked in the local textile mill and was used to strong smells
so he had no problem in close proximity to Rose. The problem
arose after her parents died and the shop became Rose's. Fred
couldn't wait to leave the mill.

'But, Fred,' Rose wailed. 'I could sell the shop. We'd be able
to buy a little bungalow and put a bit by for when we retire.'

'Rose, it's a little gold mine. Always has been. We'd be daft
to let it go. Your mother wouldn't branch out but we will. We'll
do mushy peas and how about rock salmon cakes?'

Rose silently cursed the shop. She'd be stuck with it for

the rest of her life. Then she suddenly thought of retirement. If she and Fred worked all out for another twenty-five years, they could retire at fifty.

From then on, Rose daily thrust the fish into the hot dripping and stirred the chips, dreaming all the time about what they would do with their retirement. Blackpool, a little bungalow at the select North End. New clothes, new furniture. Nothing would go into that bungalow that had any connection with a fish and chip shop.

Twenty-five years passed. Mushy peas, scampi, chicken legs. No doubt about it, Fred was really go-ahead. He even suggested buying the property next door and turning it into a fish restaurant. But Rose quickly vetoed that.

'We've enough to cope with. You'd have to get someone to look after it. And there's VAT. Besides, another five years and it'll be - Blackpool here we come!'

They retired to Blackpool with everything that Rose had promised herself as she'd dreamed amidst the fish and chips. There was also a nice little bit of capital to care for them quite pleasantly.

Rose was determined to make up for her years engulfed in an atmosphere of batter and chips and vinegar. Joyfully she went to church, knowing that she exuded Coty and not fried fish. Fred bought some golf clubs, but when he was told that the club waiting list was ten years, he reckoned at sixty, it wasn't worth the wait, so he joined a darts team.

Mrs Walker, a friendly lady who owned the greengrocer's shop, asked Rose if she would like to join the Ladies' Literary Luncheon Club. When Rose hesitated, Mrs Walker rushed to assure her that no-one was expected to be a great reader. It was called that because their first speaker had been someone called Dickens. 'But not Charles,' laughed Mrs Walker. 'We may not be spring chickens, but we're not so ancient.'

After a few Luncheon Club meetings, Rose began to sort out in her mind the various ladies. There were the retired hotel owners. They looked the most prosperous with their fur jackets and diamond eternity rings. Others had owned boarding houses, or guest houses as they preferred to call them. Some of the women had come to Blackpool from far afield, hoping to recapture the pleasures of past holidays. Some were doubtful about their decisions.

At one lunch Rose found herself seated next to a large lady who oozed confidence. The waiter handed round the menus. 'The halibut is very good today, ladies,' he whispered confidentially. It was the daily lie expected of him by the Chef.

In decided tones, Rose said, 'No fish for me. I'll have beef.'

'Are you allergic to fish then?' asked Mrs Walker. 'I've noticed you never buy it when you're in the shop.'

'No,' said Rose. 'I just ran a fish and chip shop and that's finished me for fish for the rest of my life.'

'Really,' said Mrs Walker, 'Oh, Mrs Chalmers, you had one too, didn't you?'

Mrs Chalmers raised her eyebrows and everything else, fur, pearls, bosom. 'No, I owned a fish *restaurant*, which,' and she smiled at Rose, 'is rather different to a fish and chip shop.'

There was a silence, one long enough for Rose to experience again her old hatred, only this time the fish and chips included Mrs Chalmers.

'Well, you still have to fry fish, even if it is a cafe.'

'Restaurant, dear,' cooed Mrs Chalmers.

The rest of the meal was subdued, with Mrs Walker wondering if she'd upset Rose and lost a good customer.

Mrs Chalmers obliged the Chef by having the halibut and was moved to tell the unimpressed waiter how delicious it was. 'And I should know,' she insisted. 'Only the best was served in my restaurant.'

Rose and Fred were not overjoyed when they had a phone call from Nellie, a cousin Rose hadn't seen for years.

'Last I heard, she'd gone to live at Hebden Bridge. That's typical of Nellie. We never hear anything from her till we move to Blackpool.' However, Rose felt that they couldn't very well refuse Nellie's offer to visit for a few days.

After two days of non-stop talking and catching up on the years in between, Rose remembered her Literary Luncheon. She decided to take Nellie as her guest, but thought it best to warn her about Mrs Chalmers.

'She's a right stuck-up one. Put me down 'cos we only had a fish and chip shop and she had a fish restaurant. In fact, you must have known it, Nellie. You lived in Todmorden for years before you went to Hebden Bridge, didn't you?'

'A fish restaurant? In Todmorden?' Nellie pondered. 'I don't remember one. And I knew Todmorden like the back of my hand. Fish restaurant... there was a little fish and chip shop down Hive Street, and another in Palace Road. Wait a minute, did you say Chalmers? Well, I never... it would be that shop in Palace Road. They put two tables in the window so you could rest your feet if you were waiting for extra big pieces to be fried. And if you wanted, Mrs C would do you a bit of bread and butter if you decided to eat your fish and chips there. Mind you, a lot used to say that just 'cos Millie Chalmers' shop were in Palace Street, she thought she were a bit of royalty herself.'

Rose decided that Nellie should meet Mrs Chalmers again after so long. They arrived early to be sure of seats at her table.

'This is my cousin Nellie, from Todmorden, Mrs Chalmers.'

There was a loud cry of recognition from Nellie. 'Well, I never. If it isn't Millie Chalmers from Palace Street!'

Rose felt now was the time to administer the knockout blow. 'Oh, do you two know each other? Mrs Chalmers had a fish...' But Millie Chalmers was too quick.

'Nellie. How nice to see you again. Fancy, all these years and we have to meet here. Now, how's that young man of yours? Did he ever leave his wife?'

Nellie closed her mouth. Rose too. If Nellie's face was anything to go by, Millie had dealt the *coup de grace*. Well, well. Nellie having an affair with someone else's husband. Who'd have thought it? Her pondering was interrupted by the waiter, with his whispered information from the Chef. The ladies displayed none of their usual interest in it.

Rose was left with one grain of comfort. The next time Mrs Chalmers talked about her restaurant, she would be ready with Nellie's titbit about the two tables. But somehow, she had a feeling that Mrs Chalmers had finally retired from her restaurant.

Sunday Afternoon Again

Michael Yates

HE WAS only seven years old, but Danny Keegan knew a witch when he saw one. She was tall (to him) and cruelly thin, long arthritic fingers (though he didn't know the word *arthritic)* clasped round the handle of her rubber-tipped walking stick. She always wore black: a long black frock and a shawl draped across her head like a nun's cowl. When he told his mam and dad, they laughed. It was only Mrs Croome, they said, 89 years old, and she was no witch but a great grandmother whose offspring lived as far away as Attercliffe, Dronfield and Stocksbridge. He should mind his manners when he talked about Mrs Croome.

Out of school, when he played with Terry and Denis or went with his mam to Tordof's, the nearest shop on the estate, he kept a constant look-out for the witch who lived only three doors away. At least when his mam was there, he could press against her legs, become invisible. If his mam wasn't around, he took no chances: a distant glimpse of that lean, hooded figure was enough to send him scurrying into the back garden of his parents' house (there was a ginnel with a big wooden gate and a bolt he could just about reach to keep out witches) breathless and distraught. He didn't know precisely what it was that witches did to little boys, but he knew how she must hate him for knowing what she was.

His mam and dad, like all the other grown-ups, were clever enough when it came to digging the garden, putting up fences, laying the turf on their lawns, but they lived cheerfully unaware of the danger. Their idea of danger was the traffic when he played football in the street. No great menace intruded on their lives. They could not imagine the obscene spells she surely chanted by the side of the glass-fronted grate in her living room.

It was all because of the war, this ignorance. Danny, of course, could not remember the war; he had only managed to be born in the last year of it. But it infected all the grown-ups.

When Danny's dad took him aside to lecture him on some misdemeanour, he would always begin by explaining what a lucky boy Danny was, how lucky they all were to be living in the way they did - Danny, his family, all the people on the estate. Then he would talk about the war, about nearly losing his left arm scrambling out of a burning tank in North Africa and only being here today because some good mates pulled him out and only getting back the use of his muscles (except for the last three fingers, which hardly mattered) because of the National Health, which they'd never had when he was a boy.

Everything, it seemed to Danny, was being built or rebuilt, like the half-finished street where they lived. Nothing here but fields two years ago. Everyone had just been born or miraculously reborn, and it was all because of the war. Danny, strangely older than the grown-ups, could not make them understand about witches.

Every Sunday morning, Danny's dad caught the bus all the way into Sheffield. 'I'm going down the Corner Pin,' he'd say.

The Corner Pin was a pub. Danny knew what a pub was, though he'd never been in one. There was a time, before Nan, who was Mam's Mam, had come to live with them, that Mam and Dad would go to a pub and Danny would go as well. 'Now lad,' his dad would say, 'sit ont' side of step out of people's way and I'll bring thee out some lemonade and crisps. Or would tha rather have cheese biscuits?'

He always asked for crisps. Then he'd drink the lemonade as slowly as he could, alternating each sip with a single crisp, so he could stretch it out to fill the time. Sometimes it would be okay because he'd have other kids to talk to. Then they'd stand tiptoe up against the window and try to see in. You couldn't see much because the special glass was dirty white like day-old snow, but where it said the name of the pub it was clear, so you had to get really close and screw up your eyes and look through the strokes of the letters. You'd try to see Mam and Dad in the crowd of people, but you never could. Then you'd get tired from standing on your toes.

It was a relief when Nan came because then there was always somebody to stay in the house with him. But, in any case, the outings to the pub got fewer. Even when Dad did go out these days, Mam most often stayed in. To keep Nan company, she said.

So that was a pub. That was where his dad went Sunday mornings. Always the same. He'd get up early and walk down to Tordof's for The Sunday Despatch and The People, taking Danny with him while Mam and Nan fried the breakfast. He always bought Danny some Rolo or aniseed balls, even though Mam told him not to, he'd spoil his breakfast. When they got back, they'd have egg and bacon with tinned tomatoes and Dad would do the washing up, his 'Sunday job'. Then he'd settle in the front room in his armchair and read The People. But you could tell he was waiting, waiting for it to be time.

When he'd read the paper through, he'd tear out the sports pages - the ones Mam and Nan never wanted to read - and spread them on the floor. Then he'd get his best black shoes and send Danny out to the kitchen to ask for the brush, the rag and the polish. After that, he'd lay everything out on the paper, take out the laces, turn the key on the Cherry Blossom, careful that the lid didn't fly off.

Always the same routine, dipping the brush in the polish, moving it slowly across, smearing big black gobs on the bristles. He brushed each shoe in turn in short sharp jabs and circles. Then he took the rag, spat on it ('But don't tell thee mother I'm showing thee dirty habits') and rubbed the shine in. Afterwards, he put the top back on the polish, sent Danny back into the kitchen to put it all away, rucked up the paper and threw it in the bin.

After the shoes, he'd go upstairs to wash and shave; then down again in a crisp white shirt, ironed last night by Mam, and his best blue suit. He stood by the looking glass over the mantle, brushing his thin brown hair over his forehead. Then the Brylcreem, getting his fingers right into it, and rubbing it on his scalp. His hair shone like his shoes. He combed it back and parted it, looked hard at himself, rubbed his chin and pulled a hair out of his nose which made him sneeze. He never looked at his teeth, which were false, nor at his hands, which were black and calloused from the acids he worked with at the plating shop.

'How do I look?' he'd say, and 'What time's dinner?' and to Danny: 'I'll bring thee summat back.' He checked to see his flies were done up and then he was off.

His going was a signal for the others. That was when Nan would bring out her photographs from the sideboard where she kept them in bundles tied with green ribbon. She would sit herself down on the settee and sift through them: brown men with hollow cheeks, cloth caps and whiskers stood stiffly alongside brown women against brown brick buildings, brown charabancs, brown foliage. Danny loved the strangeness of the brown world, of the days before rebuilding. Mam would stay with Nan awhile, reading the paper or chipping in with a comment as Nan reminisced. But as the morning went on, she would disappear into the kitchen to see to the meal while Danny became engrossed.

When Nan spoke of the past, flexing the muscles of her memory to encompass a childhood friend or workmate of her youth, she spoke mainly of happiness. And her happiest memories were of Grandad Guthrie, who looked, so everyone said, the spitting image of Joe Stalin.

Danny didn't know who Joe Stalin was or what he looked like, except that he looked like Grandad Guthrie, and here was a picture of Grandad, brown and broadly made, proud of himself, gazing out over a luxuriant and wicked moustache, dressed in his police inspector's overcoat with a number on the shoulder.

Nan said that Grandad Guthrie had been such a man as would walk straight across the road, looking neither right nor left, a single gloved hand raised high to warn the traffic he was not to be hindered.

When he travelled on the bus in plain clothes, a ripple of fear would run through the ranks of the criminal classes seated on the top deck. There's a D on the bus, they'd say - D being for detective, as Danny had learned at school. And also for Danny, he liked to point out.

The best of Nan's stories, though it was sad, was about the downfall of Grandad Guthrie and the unfairness of it. He was all set to become a chief inspector or something else very high up in the Sheffield police when fate dealt him a blow. That was just how Nan put it: *Fate dealt a blow*.

It had all the marks of triumph when Grandad Guthrie was chosen to be among a small welcoming party for the Prince of Wales, arriving at Victoria Station on an official visit. But when, on the day, Grandad Guthrie fell over on the platform, and a senior officer, again in Nan's words, 'smelt drink on his breath', the result was demotion, pre-empted by Grandad's decision to resign. He became a private detective.

For a while he followed husbands to hotels ('Why?' asked Danny, 'Were they burglars?') but the strange hours and other details of the trade were too much for Nan who nagged him to get more regular employment until he became a security guard at a place Nan only referred to as The Arcade.

The Arcade was a friendly place, especially to a man like Grandad Guthrie. During this period, he managed to eke out his salary with perks from those shopkeepers for whom he was prepared, it appeared, to be exceptionally alert. But Fate had a second blow to deal.

One day, as he walked past a greengrocer's shop, the street blind fell down, striking him a glancing blow on the right shoulder. Grandad Guthrie marched into the shop to deliver an angry lecture on public safety and came out five pounds the richer. But he had overreached. The greengrocer's brother-in-law was a councillor, Nan explained. So (Danny quite lost the thread of the story here) it was back to following husbands until his premature death of an unspecified internal complaint four years later.

What made Grandad Guthrie even more real to Danny was the paraphernalia of his working life, still stored in the drawer in the bottom of the wardrobe in Nan's room: a set of photographs, most of them faded, all of them numbered, of the same criminal classes, perhaps, who had called out a warning on the bus; a pair of shiny handcuffs that Danny's slender wrists easily evaded; and two truncheons - one standard issue with leather strap, the other a kind of ceremonial version in white wood with blue ribbon.

There had been another souvenir, a revolver. But Danny's Uncle Alfred had thrown it in the canal just before Grandad died. 'Why?' asked Danny, but Nan shook her head and said nothing. Danny sighed. He coveted that gun. It would have served him well against the witch.

'Show us your leg, Nan, show us the hole,' he'd always say whenever Nan looked sad, whenever story-telling failed. And she'd raise her skirt, pull down her thick left stocking and show him her own souvenir of the war, of the nights of the blitz, the hole where the shrapnel went in, a full half-inch deep, criss-crossed by little blue scars like veins in gorgonzola. Danny laughed with the excitement of it. 'You shouldn't encourage him,' Mam would say, coming in from the kitchen to discover what the laughter was about. 'You'd think we'd have better things to talk about. You'll give him nightmares.'

And Danny did have nightmares, but not about shrapnel. When he had them, he would wake up screaming and be sick on the sheets. Mam and Dad came in his room and switched on the light. Mam stroked his hair and Dad put the stained bedclothes in the bath while Danny blurted out the substance of his dream. As he grew calmer, his mam would rehearse the creed: only a dream, nothing to be scared of, nobody going to hurt you, no such thing as witches. New sheets were placed on the bed and tears gave way to exhaustion.

One time, urged on by his mam's wise words, he decided to do battle with the nightmare. He would put forth his will and conquer it. He would make himself wake up when that dark figure loomed out of the deepest shadow in the corner of his room. And at first it seemed he succeeded. Just as the witch reached out to take him in her cold hand, so he forced himself awake and her image disappeared. And he lay there in his bed with Rupert and the Dinky cars, a real boy in a real house and unafraid.

But then, as his eyes grew accustomed to the dark, he knew it had been no dream after all. She was there - sitting on the wooden chair where he kept his pile of comics, now strewn across the floor, though his mam always nagged him to keep his room tidy. The witch's lips spread wide in a horrid grin that said *now you know, now you know what's really true.*

He screamed. And his mam and dad rushed in and the light was switched on, drowning him in its suddenness. After ten breathless, screaming minutes, when they had pieced together what had happened and when even nan was awake, they had their grown-up explanation. He had only dreamed that he awoke. Or, if he had really woken up, he had gone to sleep again and the dream had started once more. But he did not believe it. He would never believe them again. They had a nerve to tell him such things.

And his dad had a nerve alright, letting the Sunday dinner spoil after Mam worked so hard. Lamb and roast potatoes. 'He likes roast potatoes,' she said, 'more than anything.' And rhubarb tart with custard. Danny and Mam and Nan finished theirs and stacked the pots in the sink. Mam put Dad's dinner back in the oven. 'It'll all go hard,' she said, ' and it was a lovely dinner.' Her face set hard like the dinner. She put the kettle on.

'Buying his friends,' said Nan and went into the front room and sat by the window, her old eyes scanning the garden and the street beyond. Danny got some comics out of the bedroom and lay on the rug at her feet. The first comic was Tarzan. He looked at the back. It said: continued next week. That was no good. He turned to Captain Marvel. Billy Batson had been turned into a baby by the mad scientist so he couldn't say *Shazam!* It came out *Goo goo goo.* He'd read that one before and it was silly.

Mam came in with the tea. She sat down and lit a cigarette. 'Here he is,' said Nan from the window. Danny ran to the door. 'Now,' said Mam to Nan, 'don't start anything.'

The back door opened with a bang and Dad came in. His face was red and smiling and Danny could smell the sweetness of the beer. He carried two brown paper bags, one with a bottle poking out. 'Lemonade,' he said to Danny, 'and ice cream. Neapolitan. For the two of us.' Danny ran into the kitchen ahead of him.

'You said you'd be back on time,' said Mam, 'the gravy's gone solid.' She took his dinner out of the oven and turned off the gas.

'I don't mind, luv.' He smiled and swayed a little.

'It's spoilt.'

'I don't mind, petal.' His smile was huge.

'It was a lovely dinner,' said Nan.

'Take your shirt off,' said Mam, 'so you don't get your food down it. And mind those trousers.'

Dad took off his jacket, tie and shirt and hung them on the back of his chair by the kitchen table. He got a towel from the hook under the sink and tucked it down his trousers. He sat there in his vest and towel, eating his dinner.

'The ice cream's melted,' said Danny.

'All the better,' said Dad.

Danny cut the ice cream block in half with the breadknife. 'Mind your fingers now,' said Mam.

He took two large glasses out of the cupboard and dropped the halves of the ice cream into them. When he poured lemonade into the glasses, it fizzed right over the top and he had to wait for it to go down before he could fill them properly.

'Sauce is empty,' said Dad.

'It's a new bottle,' said Mam.

'Not the thick,' said Dad. He didn't mean the thick brown sauce. He meant the watery black Worcester sauce.

'There's another bottle somewhere,' said Mam, 'Can't you do?'

'There's nowt left.'

'There's a drop.'

'There's nowt.'

'It's in the pantry. New bottle's in the pantry.'

Dad got up and kicked back his chair. He went across to the pantry. 'I'm partial to a drop of that sauce. Can't see it, flower.'

'Try in front of your face.'

He grunted when he saw it, took it, slammed the pantry door and sat down again. He poured some on his dinner.

Then he looked at Danny and winked. He looked wild and funny in his vest. And strong too, with thick hairy wrists and arms. Suddenly he laughed, picked up the new sauce and drank it out of the bottle. Like black beer. Danny gaped at him. He got halfway down before he stopped, put it back on the table and wiped his mouth. Danny laughed and laughed.

'I suppose you think that's clever - in front of the boy,' said Mam.

'Just what I needed, flower.' He grinned.

'It's the drink talking,' said Nan. She went out to the front room and sat by the window again.

'You'll be sick after that,' said Mam.

'What if I am, eh? What if I bloody am?' He picked up a spoon and finished off the gravy.

Mam put the rhubarb tart in front of him. 'The custard's got a skin.'

'Don't go wittling on about it, lass. I like skin.' He licked the last drop of gravy from his spoon and used it to start on the rhubarb. Mam went off into the front room and Danny followed her, flopping down on the rug next to his comics. He drank the lemonade quite quickly, then let the dregs of ice cream slide slowly into his mouth.

After a while, Dad came in, still in his vest. 'I'll wash pots before I go to bed. Danny can dry.'

'I'm reading my comics.'

'I said tha can dry. What's tha reading? Comics again? I thought thee mam told thee to read summat decent.' He turned to Mam. 'Can't he join a library or summat? Read some decent books?'

'Leave him alone,' said Mam, 'He's no trouble. I've not seen you read a book lately. Only the form book. I suppose you've had a bet.'

'A few bob, that's all. I don't like the lad reading comics at his age. Starts 'em off wrong.'

'That's one thing her father never did,' said Nan.

'Read comics?' asked Dad.

'Give his money to bookies,' said Nan.

'It's only bloody thing he didn't do from what I can

make out,' said Dad.

'It's the drink talking, that's all it is,' said Nan, 'At least he never had to buy his friends with rounds in the pub. At least he wasn't common. Oh no, people would look round...'

'How much?' asked Mam.

'Only a couple of bob,' said Dad. His smile had gone now.

'Good money after bad,' said Nan, 'It's a mug's game. That's what her father always said.'

'Leave her bloody father out of this!'

'You never win,' said Mam, 'You study form week in week out. What good does it do?'

'Scum of the earth,' said Nan, 'that's what he used to call bookies.'

Dad was talking louder now, but not quite shouting. 'Never win? What about last Easter then? What about that?'

'Last Easter? What about last Easter?' said Mam.

'You know bloody well. Twenty pounds I made. Twenty pounds on four horses!'

'Once in a blue moon,' said Nan, 'a mug's game.'

'She always gets summat when I win. The brown coat! It paid for that!''

'She never wears it,' said Nan.

'She doesn't complain *then*. Oh no, it's a different tale then!' Now he was shouting.

'She never wears it,' said Nan, 'You never take her anywhere that isn't common. Where does she get the chance to go that's half decent, where she can wear a decent coat? And what if you do win now and again? What's the good of it? That's what her father used to say. He'd got it all weighed up. You win one week, the bookies get it back the next. Of course they do! You're keeping them bookies! Keeping them in style! And you don't see it!'

Dad turned on her. 'And tha can keep out of it! It's *my* house, isn't it? It's my name ont' rent book!'

Nan got up slowly, leaned on the arm of her chair, moved painfully towards him, limping, it seemed, from the shrapnel of her life, 'You've never wanted me in this house! I've always known that! I'll not stay where

I'm not wanted!'

'Don't be silly,' said Mam, 'He doesn't mean it. It's just Sunday afternoon again.' She turned and faced him, her broad strong face flushed, strands of her straight black hair falling out of place across her forehead, 'Well, aren't you going to bed now, now that you've done your damage? Sleep it off - it's what you usually do.'

He looked at her for a moment, then his head dropped and his whole body sagged. The towel came off and fell round his ankles, revealing two gravy stains on his flies. He opened his mouth, closed it, then turned, walked out of the room and up the stairs in silence. Danny looked at Mam, but she looked away. After a moment or two, she went out to the foot of the stairs and shouted up: 'Tea's at six. It's corned beef. See you set the alarm.' Then, suddenly, everything was quiet.

With quiet determination, Danny decided to seek out the witch and destroy her. He continued to give the front of Mrs Croome's house a wide berth, but began to position himself regularly in the fields at the back, looking out for her. From his hiding place, he would study her through the windows as she filled the kettle from the kitchen tap or dusted the dresser in the bedroom.

Every time he caught her unaware like this, he would stare at her, beam all his hatred, his concentrated loathing. When he could not see her but knew her to be in the house, he would pour his malice into the brickwork, letting it seep into the walls like damp and lie there. Sometimes he would take out one of his comics - he started with the serials that nobody else wanted for swops - then lie atop the mound where he normally played mountain climbers and army men with Terry and Denis, tear the pages into little strips and let the wind take them as he prayed, apt sacrifice to the savage god of children.

After a while, rather than using his favourites - The Lone Ranger, Roy Rogers, The Ringo Kid, all complete stories in this issue - he would raid Nan's wardrobe drawer or the sideboard, take out a few pictures that he guessed she wouldn't miss, she had so many. 'Go away, witch,' he would say to himself, lying in the grass, watching the house. 'Go away, horrible witch.' And he prayed: 'Oh God, let her die! She's old anyway. I want her to die.' And when the witch responded with a puzzled glance from the window or a slight stumble on the garden path, he knew his hate had struck home.

His missions into enemy territory slowly gave him confidence. The bad dreams stopped, to the great relief of his mam and dad. Though once, when the witch was taking washing from the garden line, she raised her eyes to the mound where he lay, hidden by nettles and an old tyre, and he knew she sensed him, knew his purpose, even though she couldn't see him. Her stick tapped twice on the concrete path. Then she turned away, dragging a basket of wet sheets into the house.

One day he heard that Mrs Croome was dead. His mam didn't tell him exactly - she told his dad over tea, adding: 'She'd just turned 90, the woman with the bad face says.'

'All for the best,' said Dad, adding quickly: 'There's a world of difference between 90 and 78.' This last because just lately Nan had been inexplicably poorly and confused, muttered about losing things - photographs - and had stayed in bed for several days.

'All for the best.' A surge of pleasure shot through Danny. 'I expect Nan will die too,' he said, not noticing the shocked glances they gave him. He knew at last the indescribable joy that informed their narrow lives - the joy of having survived. He too had been through a war and won. He revelled in his new-found power.

The Big Night Out

Hilary Shields

SATURDAY night at the Royal Station Hotel. The high spot of the year. The night for which the crimplene cocktail number comes out of the wardrobe and an appointment is booked at the hairdresser's. The night for which the suit is taken to the dry cleaner's and a new tie with a crest on is bought at British Home Stores.

It is the night for which we receive a real invitation in a lick-down envelope and it's RSVP so you can tell it's grand. They have to know how many places to lay up, you see.

They have a nice function room at the Royal Station. It's got pillars and plastic palm trees and there's Wedgwood bits on the ceiling and the chairs are painted gold. You have to pretend not to notice, or folk might think you weren't used to that sort of thing. And we are. We go every year. Have done for ages - well, five years now. Since Harry got his long service watch, and we hope to keep going until he gets the carriage clock. But we've got a bit to go first. It's forty years service for the carriage clock.

They give you sherry when you arrive. That is, after you've left your coat with the lady and got the pink ticket. I gave it to Harry one year and he lost it. I had to wait till the end to get my coat - the very last one! Talk about embarrassing. And just as the lady gave me my coat, Harry found the ticket. So, since then I've put it in my little satin handbag, along with the lace hanky and the lipstick and the ten pence.

While you drink your sherry, you look about for friends. You see them, you say 'Ayup, see you're here again, hoping for the carriage clock this year?' or 'Haven't you been before? Well, I'm sure you'll enjoy yourselves. *We* always do.'

All the managers are there and it's nice for us wives to see what they look like: you can put a face to an anecdote then. So when Harry says 'I had to go and see Mr Oldfield in marketing about that,' I can picture quite a nice man, smiling and joking. Not a bit how Harry paints him.

Anyway, after half an hour, everyone moves into action.

There are long tables all laid up with white cloths and our names hand-written on little cards so we know where to sit. We mill around looking for our places, but not too eagerly. But Harry makes no secret of the fact that he's been keeping room for his meal all day, so he calls out 'Come on, Flo, here we are. This is where we're troughing.' He thinks that's funny.

Those waitresses fly round, and you get a tiny bit of soup in the bottom of the dish, three scoops and it's gone. The first ones to be served have done long before the whole table gets theirs. Next, there's a teeny bit of fish in sauce, always with two bones which you have to deal with politely. And then comes a roast. It isn't like a roast you do yourself, its always a bit grey. But there's chips and boiled with it, and two sorts of veg. Out of a tin, but never mind. They follow that with gateau. Harry is shameless. He always says to the waitress 'If anyone doesn't want theirs, send it my way, Miss.' But by that time, she's five people away, dealing out plates of gateau like a pack of cards. Oh... and you get wine with the main course. They come round, 'Red or white? Red or white?' Though the men invariably say 'Bring us a beer when you can, love.'

Well, you can relax after the gateau. They bring coffee and mints, and the Managing Director gets on his feet at the top table and makes a speech.

'Ladies and gentlemen, we are all here to enjoy ourselves this evening and to honour the men who have kept this firm going over the years, to make this whole thing possible. Some of them have been with us since 1944. And don't forget! If it were not for people like that, giving loyalty to the company all their lives, then there would be no Twenty-five Year Club, and probably no factory at all! It is to them that we owe thanks that we all have a job to come to. May I ask you to join with me in wishing them all many, many more years, both with the company and in their well-earned retirement?' (Applause.) 'The following have this year joined our numbers by serving twenty-five years, and it is a great pleasure to present them with their watches.' Then he reads out a list of names. (Applause). 'And now, ladies and gentlemen, I am very honoured to name the members of the Forty Year Club. Er... rather less of them.' (Laughter.)

Maybe two or three old fellows toddle up to get the carriage clock. You feel good for them. They've put in enough time, God knows. Getting up and going to work, cycling through the rain, man and boy, never worked anywhere else.

Then the band starts up. Immediately the keen ones get on the dance floor, the ones who learned to dance when dancing was dancing. Those who aren't dancing draw their chairs together to talk, though you have to shout over the music.

You meet some interesting people. There's the man who always says 'I'd ask you to dance my dear, but I've got this wooden leg. Got caught in a press in 1952.' And the one who can remember when Thomas Ward's had an elephant in the yard to move steel bar about. Poor thing. There's a man who's worked in the casting shop all his life, never been promoted but didn't mind because he knew the work. Sad, really.

Well, if I nudge Harry hard enough, he will dance with me. Just the once. What's the point in going to a dinner dance if all you get is a dinner? By this time, he'll be well into his third pint, but he can manage a foxtrot if I push him a bit.

I like to see who's dancing and what they're wearing. You get all sorts. One year, a lady came in a purple crochet dress with lurex in it. She didn't half suffer with the heat. It's funny the variety you get, considering everyone is dressing in their best. There's long and short and backless, and some with sleeves. And all colours. In fact, anything goes.

Well, as the evening wears on, it gets less formal, until just about everyone is on the dance floor doing *The Birdie Song*. They always follow it with *Agadoo doo doo*, and of course at the end, *The Last Waltz* with a singer at the microphone pretending it's romantic to be going home with a husband who's six pints up. He should try it. We end with *Auld Lang Syne* and finally the National Anthem. You feel silly standing to attention on the spot where you've just been shaking pineapples from the tree. So you scuffle in your handbag for that pink cloakroom ticket - won't be caught out this year and hurry off so you'll be early in the queue.

'Bye Jim, Mary, Rita, George, Joyce, Mr and Mrs Wilkinson. That were a right good do. See you same time, same place next year.'

My Great-Grandad Had a Farm

Mark Turner

SUNSHINE. Like a great desert, the road leads back to you. Sunshine comes rolling over the hill on this fat summer's morning with the promise of a thousand babies. The road leads from me to you, you carry it all on your back, quiet man, with children's voices dancing round your feet. My dad and my dad's brother and my grandad coming up the hill, laughing and telling stories. And they'd walk down Mary Pannell and back to Castleford. The sun rises. Ledston washed in a green shock. And the sun is the sound of children laughing, same road, same direction. Dad's brother, grandad... no, further back, when there was a farm, that's where it happened. On that farm my great-grandad pulled eleven children out of his wife, held them up to the sun and pointed, shouting, 'This is ma sun! Ma sun!' And smiled a smile like the splitting skin of an orange.

Florence played by the water butt. She was told not to. Great-grandad Proud was in the cattle shed, milking cows. Sweat hung on his brow. Between his fingers and thumb, milk pissed into the milking can. Florence played by the water butt; she was told not to play by the water butt. Nine children, Florence's brothers and sisters, had been wiped out with tuberculosis. She saw their little milky faces ripple in the cold water where her delicate hand traced, until they quickly disappeared and she brought her hand back with a start from the face of Great-grandad Proud.

'But I told her not to play in the water butt,' he said to his wife who was nursing Florence.

'You should not hit the child - she's too young to under-stand.'

He struck up his pipe, 'There's diseases round the farm, and in the water butt. I told her not to play in the water butt.'

When Florence was ninety-one, she lived alone in a bun-galow in Halfacres, Castleford. And when she came to our house for Sunday dinner, she couldn't see the wine glass, she couldn't hear mother repeat 'One or two potatoes?' and had little appetite for Co-op beef. But how she remembered my great-grandad's farm and her beautiful mother with straight, long blonde hair, right blonde it was. And her brother and sister that survived. And her father, my great-grandad, and his temper. What a temper, wicked, wicked. And the apples and the plums and the blackberries and young lads and lasses a-courting, proper mind. And always a pig cut up for table; that's when pork was pork. And her mother plaiting her hair right down her back; like corn it was, like corn. And she had a dog that Great-grandad Proud beat to death with a pick, because of his temper. 'But the pork, the bacon,' she'd say chewing on a bit of beef. That's when pork was pork. All gone now, all gone. Dead, dead, dead.

One day a man came down from the North wanting to buy land, and before he left he shook Great-grandad Proud's hand. He came into the waiting darkness of the kitchen and the waiting darkness of his wife and children. 'Man's come down from the North. Reckons on he'll buy. I've worked this farm too long, had enough.' His eyes in his back were watching her. 'We're going to Castleford in the morning.'

Some days later, Great-grandad Proud, his wife, little Flo, her brother and sister perched on top of an open cart with all their world, to Castleford Town came.

Every Friday night when the Butty Boys paid out at the miners' club, some stayed, one pint of beer leading to another. Many folk would see them tipped off the back of a cart outside the brick backs, and wives left to pick up pieces.

Great-grandad Proud got himself a job down the pit. 'Easy for a farmer's son,' he said, as his hands grasped on a shovel and pick with a bit of spit. 'Easy for a farmer's son.'

Great-grandad Proud walked to the public house, where the Butty Men were, for his money. He drank a pint of beer then stood in the queue, right awkward like, for he was a farmer really. He answered to his name and they put coppers in his hand. Their eyes met and fused in silence. Was he about to cry or perhaps kill someone?

'Got a problem, Proud?' asked the Butty Man.

His mouth cracked, thinking for something to say. 'Not enough, not paid enough.'

'That's your wage, Proud. Take it and be on your way.'

Great-grandad Proud lifted up the table, Butty Men and all and tipped them to the floor, with penny farthings and half pennies shattering all over. Then he left.

'Where's your husband, Missis?'

There were bobbies at the door. Little Flo hid behind her mother's apron, her eyes wide and listening. 'Minding his own business, I expect.' There were two of them and they looked ready. Little Flo and her mother stood in the doorway. Then they went.

One day there was an accident down the pit and Great-grandad Proud copped for it. His leg not broken but smashed. He wouldn't go home in the ambulance. 'I'll walk by meself,' he said. He must have been daft, he must have been pissed. When the prop cracked, he just smiled. I says 'Is thy alright?' And he just smiled. So I thought fuck ye, ye cunt. He walked home with his smashed leg in agony and gangrene set in. Up above was a full moon that shone on the silence of the hedges and the little lanes. He didn't mean it to end like that. He didn't mean to drink like that and he was sorry.

'Tha'll get a job in The Ship, Florence, when tha's thirteen. Tha'll clean spittoons and wait on Flo. I'll see thee right. I'm a farmer's boy, no bloody miner. No bloody preacher can take me out of my mine to the gates of heaven to lead me to the baby Jesus. No bloody preacher. I'm a farmer's boy, a farmer's boy!'

Perhaps he had a vision of a great cloud bursting in a desert; red, ballooning into something almost beautiful, that put out the sun, that grieved in little tears and settled on a baby's face. This was his sun. 'Ma sun! Ma sun!' And a thousand babies slept on little white stones, softly smiling, because they had not been born. And he saw the whole world cave in to his little farm, and pigs and duck eggs in long sharp grass. And milky faces of his little ones smiling in the water butt, and Flo's hand washing ripples across his brow. And he came into the water, a black pool that travelled into infinite time; and he died.

Flo caught herself a fella. And they went a-courting down the lanes of Fairburn and Ledston. He loved walking, did Flo's fella, and they called him Cecil. He'd got himself a good job down pit. He was smart; smartest man in town, best suit in town, and his shoes always shone like berries. He didn't drink, didn't smoke and he'd saved a bob or two.

One day he proposed to her, asked for her hand in wedlock. They got married and went to Blackpool, and ate oysters on the pier. Flo spat it out, said it was horrible, not worth a penny-farthing. Cecil paid a man to take a photograph. Everyone stood around and watched as she held his hand and glowered, proud of Cecil in his black ribboned hat and his black suit. Cecil smiled, proud of Flo; then snap.

They had two beautiful babies that they christened Clifford and Geoffrey. When Clifford, her first, was born, he was the most beautiful baby in the world. Wherever he went, people would look at him in the pram and say so.

Clifford fought in Burma. They did not hear from him for three years. They thought he was dead; Florence shrunk to a corpse. Then one day, after we'd won the war, he came back, and he was there looking just like a skeleton.

Geoffrey was my father. He was in the Air Force in Egypt. The Arabs hated him and spat at him in the street. My father was a wireless operator with ear phones. He sent morse code messages to bombers overhead. This is how it went - *didi, di, da, da, dididi, di, da, didi, di.* He'd tap it out on my head, then we'd watch it after Sunday dinner; bombers over Germany, the Battle of the River Plate, Hitler and his gang of cut-throats, Lord Haw Haw with a funny voice saying, 'This is Germany calling, this is Germany calling'. And I'd chase upstairs to my dad's little wireless and ear phones, and on the little tapper it would be World War Two again - *didi, di, dadada, didi, dididi, dadada, di, di, dididi, dada, didi, di...* getting no further than the little specks of rain freckles on the window. When from across backs comes the '60s and pop music for the teeny-boppers and pop pickers and *Ow's about that then?*

Florence lived on and on and on, until she couldn't get out any more, so we bought her a budgie for company. Her hair fell out at eighty-five through nerves; she was almost bald. At ninety it suddenly grew back, a full head of thick black hair. The doctor couldn't believe it. Florence put it down to Schofield's Neats Foot Oil. All day she sat brushing it in and swearing by Schofield's Neats Foot Oil. The oil stank, but it smelt nice on her. When she was ninety-two, she got dizzy and kept falling over, so we put her in a home.

One morning she fell and broke her hip. She had an operation, steel pins and traction. I think they thought she'd die. They gave her a walking frame and sent her back to the home. No matter how cross the Matron got, she couldn't walk to the dining room and they said it was not their job to push her. So that was that. They put her to bed on her back and she died of pneumonia some days later.

We gathered at Uncle Cliff's for the funeral. The Funeral Director came into the lounge and gently whispered, 'Don't stand too close to the grave when they are lowering her down - you might fall in.' It had been raining all week and the grave diggers had had a terrible time digging Florence's grave. She always said she'd drag us all down with her when she went.

We were all huddled around her. It was winter and we felt the coldness of the earth. The dry words of the preacher were lost in the wind. On the skyline, a cold steel blue, was Ledston and Fairburn where a long time ago my Great-grandad had a farm. And the road stretched way back to the sun as big as a desert with the promise of a thousand babies. Ledston and Fairburn sun soaked in a green shock. And pigs and plums, and little Flo dreaming by the water butt, and her mother with her hair like corn. The little children; all of her brothers and sisters. Young lads and lasses a-courting, proper mind. And always a fresh cut pig for table. She kept good table. When pork was pork. Gone now, all gone; dead, dead, dead.

Sometimes, when we are very frightened, we think 'This is it!' And an overwhelming nausea rises from the ground, and we are alone, and what we need is a miracle. Something to happen out of nothing. Something that trips an odd beat and says 'Stop!' Like little drops of water settling on the frame and falling to the sill in spilt rain - *didi, dida, da, da, didi, di...* and I remember messages over Germany, the farm, my father in Egypt, Clifford in Burma, Florence and Great-grandad Proud. It must mean something. Long distant messages getting through just in time - *didi, di, dadada, didi, dididi, di, dadada, didi, didi, di, da, didi, dididi, di, da, da, da, didi, dididi, di, dadada.*

Stringy Billy

Frank Worsdale

DOT Cantrill was eleven. She was short, stocky and tough. A shock of black hair crowned her cheeky, cheerful, but wise-looking features. Her Little Gang (older kids were in the Big Gang) was made up of eight to ten year olds - mostly boys. They didn't see Dot as a girl. They saw her as their leader.

Dot had gained fame in the back street of Streatfield Crescent, up the backs, when she led raids against Foljambe Crescent, the backs next to them.

Foljambe's Little Gang always broke ranks and fled in terror when Dot led her stone-throwing troops on sorties - sometimes as far as a hundred yards into enemy territory where there was always the danger of counter attack from Foljambe's Big Gang.

Anyway, it was Sunday morning and raids on Foljambe were strictly for later in the day.

The July sun rose higher and dampness from an overnight shower evaporated from the red roofs of the pit houses. The bell-man came round on his bicycle. 'Take notice, take notice... A general meeting of mineworkers WILL be held at eleven o'clock in the Welfare Hall. Business IMPORTANT.'

His cry echoed around the terraced houses and served, along with the clanging of the Catholic Church bell, to remind colliers, sleeping off their Saturday night drink, that Sunday morning had come.

Only three of Dot's gang were out. They mimicked the well known message in time with the bell-man. 'Cheeky sods!' he said as an automatic response, then he carried on ringing his hand bell and bellowing his Welfare Hall invitation as yapping dogs accompanied him down Foljambe Crescent.

'Where are we going?' Titch Hilton ventured to ask his leader.

'Let's go down Stringy Billy's,' answered Dot.

Stringy Billy's was a lane in the old village named after

a deformed and retarded boy who in summer sat in the lane outside his home playing with string - lots of string.

'I'm not going past Stringy Billy again. Last time he nearly got hold of me,' protested Titch.

'Yer scared,' said Dot.

Then, after a few exchanges of 'y'are scared,' 'I'm not scared,' Titch capitulated.

'All right then, but I'll have to ask me mam first.'

After clearance from his mam, and acquisition of a two pound jam jar intended for bringing home tiddlers and sticklebacks, Titch, Dot, Tony and Vaccie Roy Mullins, an evacuee from Croydon, set off.

Dot was wearing a shirt, long blue serge skirt and black pumps with frayed toes; the lads were in knee-length short trousers with braces, shirt sleeves rolled up and, of course, black pumps - these purchased for one and threepence and only two clothing coupons from the Friday market. It was a hot day, socks were not necessary.

The four ran, walked and dawdled, climbed on walls and swung on gates. For a minute they sat on the steps of The Royal under the big red magnet sign. They said 'Ayup' to a group of miners in best suits, flat caps and white silk scarves who squatted, waiting for opening time. Then the gang were off again.

At the Hippodrome a picture of Laurel and Hardy dressed as soldiers in 'The Doughboys' attracted them. While they were studying the picture, a squad of the village's own doughboys, the Local Defence Volunteers, marched past and the four stood to attention and gave mock salutes.

Over the school field they skipped. Dot would be in the senior girls' after the holidays, the other three were still juniors. They took a special delight in weaving across the empty school yard with no fear of teachers. In the school field they ran along the top of the mound covering the air raid shelters and did roly-polies down its warm grass slopes.

When they reached the level crossing dividing the new mining village from the old village, the gates were closed and the four had to wait. Clinging to the creosote-smelling fence, they watched as the train plunged through, hissing, snorting and rattling away into the distance. Then the signalman turned his big wheel and the gates clattered open for the green bus and the cars and Dot's gang to cross.

Tony said, 'I'm going to drive one of them when I grow up.'

Dot, already knowing something of the limitations placed on girls and with a vague feeling of envy, told him, 'You can't. You'll have to go down the pit - 'cos yer Dad's at pit, see.'

They ran across the sleepered crossing, entered the old village and walked under the elm trees as far as the police station. There they sat in the shade for a while on a rusting iron grille seat, swinging their legs . Roy occupied himself by spitting down through the grille at ants busy below.

Stringy Billy's lane was just opposite the Police Station but nobody seemed eager to be first to go across. Dot took a drink from a pop bottle of water and gave the others a swig.

'Come on, we'll go now. Keep close to me,' ordered Dot.

They left the shade of the trees, crossed the road and walked in a single file. Titch at the rear kicked up dust from the hard-packed track of the lane.

Willowherb grew around the laneside ditch and their pink flowers attracted the bees. Titch, to delay progress to the place where he knew Billy would be sitting, caught a bee in his bare hands. He held it to Tony's ear.

'It's a red-bum,' he said, 'it don't sting.'

They all listened to the buzzing from within Titch's cupped hands, pleased to be distracted from the thought of the coming confrontation with Stringy Billy.

'He's there,' Dot hissed as they rounded the slight bend. 'Keep in.'

Stringy Billy, strapped in his home-made pushchair fixed on old pram wheels, had been pushed right to the garden gate. The gang would have to pass within two or three yards of him.

The four youngsters kept as close as they could to the

hawthorns on the side of the lane furthest away from Billy. Their usual gang confidence had faded and they walked on in tense silence.

Billy was making gurgles and throaty noises. When they dared to lift their eyes to look closely, they saw that his pushchair had tipped. It was leaning over at a dangerous angle. Billy's claw-like hand clutched the fence as he tried to stop his chair from toppling over completely.

'What'll we do?' said Tony.

'Leave him. It's a trick,' was Dot's command.

Billy's mouth slavered. He looked distraught.

'Yer can't leave him like that,' said Roy, daring to contradict his leader.

Dot, who liked to specially impress Vaccie Roy, pondered. Then the courage that had gained her fame in the raids on Foljambe surged and she said, 'We'd better pull him up then, hadn't we?'

Roy, knowing he'd only himself to blame, reluctantly went to help. Once he saw that Billy hadn't harmed his friends, Tony also stepped forward to give a hand. Titch stood back. He still wouldn't believe that Billy wasn't a monster who caught and tied his victims up with string.

As the three righted the chair and set it straight, Billy gawped a toothy smile and made guttural noises. He was excited. His eyes shone and, like a friendly dog, his whole being vibrated his appreciation at being rescued by the gang.

Dot was smitten. She had never felt that caring feeling so strongly before - not even the time when she accidentally dropped her baby brother. She picked up Billy's rabble of string and put it in his hand. Again Billy sounded his 'gurrr-gurrr' and smiled his wide open smile. Billy's mother, hearing the commotion, came down the garden path.

'He fell over, missus,' Dot explained. Then, without thinking, added, 'Can we take him a walk?'

Understanding what had been said, Billy jerked back and forward in his chair and gurgled to indicate that he'd like that. His mother looked Dot over, looked at the boys and then agreed.

'But only as far as the river, mind. And be careful.'

Dot and Roy took the chair handles and, with Tony and Titch at left and right manhandling from the chair arms, they pushed Billy along. He wasn't very heavy.

Titch, gaining in confidence, deliberately touched Billy's thin arm as he pushed. 'Wonder if he'd like to listen to a red-bum?' he said to Dot. But Dot didn't seem to hear.

They wobbled Billy in his chair down to the lane end, through the big buttercup field and up to the wooden bridge that spanned the River Torne and led to the golf-links.

Dot stood on the bridge, holding the chair handles and watching Billy. Down below, her gang busied themselves paddling and trying to coax tiny fish into the jam jar.

The sun was high and hot, the Torne's low rippling waters corrugated the sun's reflection and yellow buttercups shimmered in the haze. On the golf-links side of the river, cows ruminated lazily and half-heartedly swished away the flies with their tails.

At that moment, Dot didn't mind not being free to play in the river. For the first time she didn't mind not being able to lead her gang and tell them what to do. She looked at Billy's thin, twisted body and pathetic eyes. She looked at the twig-like fingers entwining his mess of string and she felt that being there with Billy, on the wooden bridge under the warm sun, was perfect.

Titch caught some sticklebacks. He put pebbles and watercress in the jar to make them feel at home. He showed them to Billy. Billy bumped up and down and quivered with joy when he saw the fish prodding and mouthing against the side of the jam jar.

After Dot thought half an hour might have passed, the four pushed Billy home, through the big buttercup field and up the lane named after their important friend.

Billy's mother was pleased to have had her son taken care of for a while and asked the children to come again sometime. As a reward she held out a baking tray and presented each of the four with a jam tart.

'It's like getting a medal, isn't it?' said Titch, half

thinking that he might take the tart home to show his mam. But when he saw the others licking away at the jam, he ate his as well.

Surrounded by his mother and four new friends, Billy was filled with a jumpy happiness. He gurgled and rocked when Titch held up the fish to show the mother. As the gang waved and left, he sat staring and still till they went out of sight. Then he resumed his preoccupation with his string.

Near the police station the gang met Joyce and Olive Finch from Streatfield Crescent. They tried to tell them that they'd taken Stringy Billy for a walk. The sisters just wouldn't believe it.

A train was coming. The level crossing gates clanged closed and again they had to wait. For the second time that day, Tony announced that he was going to be a train driver. This time, instead of denying him, Dot, still thinking of frail Billy and his big brown eyes, answered, 'I'm going to be a nurse when I grow up - so I can look after people.'

After the great train shuddered through and vanished in its swirling shroud of steam, the four made their way home through the village. It was a long time since they'd set off but there still seemed an unending stretch of that sunny day ahead of them.

'Where we going this after?' asked Tony.

Dot kicked a tin can out of her way. Then, as the Indians do before attacking cowboys, she did a little dance. Then she gave a whoop and said, 'Let's raid Foljambe.'

Postman's Knock

Jean Pearson

THERE it was again. The long brown envelope that had just dropped in through the letter box was getting to look a little too familiar. She'd ignore it today, leave it alone, pretend it wasn't there.

She knelt on the mat by the front door, picking out the other bits and pieces that had accompanied the brown envelope, taking care that her fingers didn't even touch the paper.

'Damn the thing,' she said, 'I can't see it.'

She rose from her knees and, carefully striding over the offending envelope, went through to the kitchen. A boring lot, she thought, throwing the assortment onto the kitchen table.

'I know what you all are without even opening you,' she said to the letters scattered on the table top. She turned towards the door. 'Including you!' she shouted, then, remembering she was ignoring it, turned to fill the kettle.

She spent most of the morning pretending it wasn't there. She even vacuumed around it. That was tricky. For a moment, she thought it was going to get sucked in till she kicked it away with her slippered foot.

When the milkman called for his money and pointed it out to her, he gave her a funny look when she said, 'What letter?'

By lunchtime, she thought it all a bit silly so she picked it up and shoved it in a drawer. It would be easier to ignore there.

Rita came round after her husband Tom had gone back to work. 'I saw the postman come,' she said in a conspiratorial voice. 'Did he bring a you-know-what again?'

'No, I don't know what, Rita. I've decided they don't exist.'

'But you can't do that, Sheila. You can't just pretend it's not happening. Did one come again?' she persisted.

'Well, if you must know, yes.'

'Where is it then? Come on, let's have a look!'

'I've not even opened it. I've told you, I'm ignoring them from now on.'

'Oh, come on, Sheila. How can you sit there saying that?'

'Quite easy, I've had enough.'

Rita was Sheila's best friend. They never kept secrets from each other and Rita was going to make sure it stayed that way.

'Where have you put it then?'

Sheila leaned over to switch on the television, making a show of not hearing her.

'Come on, Sheil, where have you put it?'

'If you must know, it's in the drawer.'

Rita's eyes lit up. 'Can I get it?'

'Am I going to be able to stop you?'

Rita jumped up and crossed over to the sideboard. She touched the top drawer with her long red painted fingernail.

'It's this drawer, isn't it?' Rita had the letter out in a flash. 'Come on, open it up. I'm dying to see what's in this one.'

'I've told you, Rita, I'm not touching it.'

'Alright.' Rita put the letter on top of the sideboard and made to return to her chair. Then she stopped, looking back at the brown envelope, which seemed to mesmerise her. 'Well, can I open it then?'

'On your head be it, Rita,' Sheila said. 'On your head be it.'

Rita grabbed the envelope, holding it close to her substantial bosom and sat down. She giggled like a schoolgirl as she turned the envelope over and over in her hands before inserting a long red fingernail beneath the sealed flap.

'Are you sure you don't want to do it, Sheila?' she asked, waving the offending article under her nose.

'How many more times, Rita? I'm not interested.'

Rita returned to the task of opening the letter, deliberately taking her time and rolling her eyes at Sheila.

'Stop that, Rita, do you know how daft you look?'

'Spoilsport.'

The letter was open, Rita's hand went into the envelope

and drew out the folded sheet of foolscap. She waved it under Sheila's nose again.

`It won't bite you. Do you want me to read it out to you?'

'Don't you dare. I've told you, I'm not interested.'

Sheila was beginning to look upset and Rita suddenly felt mean. She slid the letter back into the envelope.

'I'm sorry, love, I thought you were kidding. I didn't realise you were so bothered by it.'

'Oh, forget it. It's just me being daft. Look, read the damn thing out and let's get it over. I don't suppose it'll be any different from the others.'

By the time Dennis came home from work, Sheila had regained her composure. Rita had gone home to get the kids ready for bed and the letter was with the others, under the lining paper in her dressing table drawer.

'What have you got planned for tonight then, Sheila?' The last chip disappeared down Dennis' throat as he spoke.

'Rita wanted me to go to one of those party plan things up the road - but I'm not bothered. I can get what I want from the shop. Are you going out?'

'Me and Tom thought we might go out for a pint if that's okay with you, love?'

'As long as it's not midnight when you come home.'

'As if I would, love.'

Dennis rose from the table, scraping his chair back on the kitchen floor.

'Why don't you go across and keep Rita company?'

'She's been here nearly all afternoon. I don't think we've anything left to say.'

'Gerron. I'm sure you'll think of something.'

During the last couple of weeks, Sheila had noticed that Dennis was taking a lot of care with his appearance for his nights out with Tom. Always a shower and a clean shirt, always a shave and some Aramis.

'Stop it, Sheila,' she told herself. 'He's always been smart. What's so different now?'

If she was honest with herself, she knew what was making her suspicious, and the daft thing was it had nothing to do with Dennis. It was those awful letters.

'I'm off, love,' he called as he went out of the front door. 'Won't be late.'

Now what do I do, she thought. Sit here and fall asleep in front of the telly, go to Rita's, or what? She picked up the evening paper from the settee where Dennis had left it, and turned to the television page. All talky-talkies, she thought, nothing here to tempt me. One thing was tempting her though - the thought of the letters hidden away upstairs. She'd never really looked at them properly, not by herself. Rita was always with her when she opened them. Rita, giggling like a daft schoolgirl, making her more embarrassed. She decided to go upstairs and have another look while the house was quiet.

Why hadn't she thrown the silly things out? Why had she kept them? Rita would have something to say if she knew she was hoarding them instead of tearing them up like she'd said. How many now? She spread them out on the bed. Six with today's.

She scoured the envelopes for clues, though they'd already done that as each one was delivered. All posted in town, first class, always the same cheap brown envelopes and always typed. If I was a detective, I could test for finger prints, she thought. But then realised it wouldn't help much because she hadn't any to compare them with.

The letters had been coming for about three weeks. She opened the first one thinking it was a circular. But when she'd read the contents, she couldn't believe her eyes. As soon as she knew Rita would be at home on her own, she'd rushed across, bursting in the kitchen door just as Rita was sorting the washing. She'd thrust the letter into her hands and stood back, waiting for a reaction. Rita read it twice before looking up.

'Who's sent you this?' she asked.

'How do I know? They've not bothered to sign it.'

'You must have some idea - he obviously knows you.' Rita handed the letter back.

'I've no idea, why should I? If I knew the fellow, do you think I'd be showing you?'

Rita turned to fill the kettle. 'This is a real stunner, isn't it? But what's the use writing you a letter like that if he doesn't put his name on? Do you want a coffee?'

'I thought you were washing.'

'That can wait. We've got to sort this out first.' Rita picked up all the clothes from the kitchen floor and shoved them back into the laundry basket.

'Has Dennis seen it?'

'It's only just come.'

'Will you show it him?'

'Don't be daft. This is going in the bin when I get home.'

But it didn't, did it? thought Sheila. She'd hidden it away in her drawer, well underneath her jumpers where Dennis couldn't accidentally find it - and the others had followed.

It had been a joke when they'd first started arriving. She even suspected that Rita had been a bit jealous. But when they kept coming, Rita's interest grew as Sheila had become more uneasy.

'You know what, Sheil,' Rita had said after the fourth, 'I really think he's serious. I don't think he could make up such stuff if he wasn't.'

'Don't be daft, Rita. What fella do I get near enough to have that sort of effect on? Anyway, if he were genuine, he wouldn't hide behind a typewriter, would he?'

'Well, he's married, isn't he? At least you know that.'

'I'm married as well and he knows that too.'

'Eh, kid,' suggested Rita, 'what if it's that blond body builder that keeps jogging down the lane every night. I bet you wouldn't think twice if it were him.'

'I don't know where you get your ideas from - and Dennis'd go mad if he knew.'

Rita laughed. 'It might do him good, Sheila. I bet he wouldn't be nipping down to the pub every night if he knew what kept dropping through your letter box.'

But this last letter had really worried her. This chap was threatening to leave his wife because of her, and she didn't even know who he was.

'It's obvious his wife's a bad 'un,' said Rita.

'How do you make that out?'

'Think about it. A chap wouldn't be living in such a dream world if his wife looked after him properly, now would he?'

'I feel sorry for her, whoever she is. Fancy your husband dreaming about another woman and not knowing anything about it.'

'Don't be so naive, Sheila. Of course she'll know something's wrong and it's obvious she doesn't care.'

'Well, I hope he doesn't send any more. If he knows me as well as he says he does, he'll know I love Den - that we're happy together.'

'Come on, it makes life exciting. Don't say you aren't enjoying them.'

'It was funny at first, but not any more. He's getting too carried away now.'

'Well, I'm enjoying them anyway. A bit of romance to start the day, what could be better? I wish he'd send me one now and again.'

'You can have 'em, Rita. I've got all the romance I want from Dennis.'

Sheila pushed the letters back under her jumpers. Whoever he was, he had got her into a state of daydreaming. Even waiting for the postman, if she were honest with herself. And that's what she found most disturbing. She had never questioned it before, but was there really enough romance in her life?

Dennis had started encouraging her to go out on her own of an evening. After he finished his tea every night, he asked her 'What have you got planned for tonight, love?' She now realised that it was just to give him an excuse to go out.

'Look, if anyone's being unfaithful, it's me,' she told herself. 'Even if it's only in my head.'

She wasn't expecting another letter the next day. There were usually a few days between each one, so when the letter box snapped and she went into the hall to fetch the mail, her heart nearly stopped. She picked up the brown envelope first this time and took it into the living room. She opened it with the brass letter opener that was normally used as an ornament.

'I'll read it before Rita comes,' she told herself, 'and in future, I'll burn them as they come without opening them first.'

The letter worried her. 'Please meet me,' he begged, 'just the once. You'll know who I am as soon as you see me.'

She was still sitting in the chair, letter on her lap, when Rita came over an hour later. She handed the letter to Rita, who sank onto the settee to read it.

'Rita, what am I going to do? Have you seen what he says at the bottom?'

Rita scanned the page, eyes flashing from one line to another. 'What? Where?'

'He says if I don't meet him, he'll come round here tonight when Dennis goes out. What am I going to do?'

'Simple, Sheila.' Rita handed the letter back. 'You'll have to go. The poor fella's obviously pining away for you.'

'How can I? The man's got a wife - and for all I know, he could be Jack the Ripper.'

'Simple. I'll come with you. You'd be safe then.'

'But would he identify himself if I had company?'

'I would follow you, out of sight. He'd never know.'

'Oh, Rita, I daren't,' wailed Sheila.

'Okay, but wouldn't you rather face him and put a stop to it than risk him coming here?'

'Put like that, I've not much option, have I?'

'And you might even fancy him when you see him. Exciting, isn't it?'

After he'd finished his tea, Dennis stretched and got up from the table. She was waiting for the inevitable question.

'What have you got planned for tonight then, love?'

Her cheeks began to burn and she turned her back to him, noisily clearing the table. 'Oh, me and Rita thought we'd go over to Betty Marsden's. She's just had twins, you know.'

'Oh well, you won't mind if I go out with Tom for a drink then, will you, as stay in by myself.'

Dennis was out of the house in just under the hour. She watched through the window as he went across the road until Tom came out. They strode up the street together, like a couple of stags, dressed to kill.

She had half an hour if she was to go through with the plan. She'd worried about how to dress and make-up. Make an effort and it'll look as if I'm encouraging him, she thought. But her pride didn't want him to be disappointed in her.

Rita called for her, coming in through the door in a haze of heady perfume.

'Eh, it's me that's got the date,' Sheila laughed nervously.

'If we go for a drink after, I might get lucky, eh?'

Sheila was having second thoughts. 'I shouldn't be doing this, should I? Think about that man's poor wife.'

'It's not your fault her husband's fallen for you. She should have looked after him better. Make the most of it, girl, it could still be that blond body builder.' She was still laughing as they went for the bus.

'Meet me in that new coffee bar at the corner of Bright Street,' he'd said in the letter. At least he hadn't asked her to walk into a pub on her own. She was silent on the journey into town, listening to Rita speculate on every possible aspect of the forthcoming meeting.

'Look, if you fancy him, Sheil, don't worry about me. I'll be okay. You go off and enjoy yourself. You know your secret'll be safe with me.'

'I'll be five minutes, Rita. That's all it's going to take. I'm going to put a stop to this once and for all.'

'Enjoy yourself. You know what they say about stolen fruit.'

'To hear you talk, Rita Prentice, anyone would think you made a habit of gadding off. It's a good job I know different.'

They separated just before Bright Street. Rita made a good job of being discreet.

Sheila's heart was thumping by the time she reached the door of the coffee shop. She stood a minute, peering in at the window, but she couldn't see anyone she recognised. The place was almost empty. She opened the door slowly, the warmth met her, increasing the fire in her cheeks. She planned to sit at a table by the door. Rita could keep an eye on her there.

She sat down facing the door and nervously picked up the menu. If she paid for her coffee before he came in, she wouldn't be beholden in any way. Just as she was giving her order to the thin young girl, Tom walked in.

Dennis will be behind him, she thought, panic rising. Now what do I do? She kept her head down while she fumbled in her purse for her money.

'Hello, Sheila, anybody sitting here?'

Keep calm, she told herself. 'I thought you were with Dennis. Where is he?'

'Dennis is okay, I'm just his alibi. It's you I need to see.'

The colour drained from her face. 'Tom! You!'

As he reached out across the table for her hand, she looked up quickly and saw Rita's face glued to the window. 'Oh, my God! This is crazy!'

Panicking, she grabbed for her bag and stood up.

'Just five minutes, Sheila, that's all I want, then you can tell me to get lost.'

'You can get lost now, Tom Prentice. Rita's outside watching all this.'

Tom looked as if she had struck him. 'You're kidding! What did you bring her for?'

'I didn't know who I was meeting, did I? Rita's my friend. She came to keep an eye on me.'

Tom let go of Sheila and she pushed her way towards the door and out. Now what was going to happen? She knew Rita's temper and could imagine the scene that was going to follow - with her in the middle of it. She stood on the pavement outside the coffee bar, Tom close behind her.

'Where is she?' he asked, breathing heavily down her neck.

'She was here a minute ago, at the window.'

The street was empty except for a taxi turning at the top. Tom took her elbow and began to propel her up the street. Sheila pulled away from him.

'I don't know about you, Tom. I'm going home and I suggest you do the same.'

They hurried towards the bus station, Sheila's mind a

tormented muddle. 'And where did you say Dennis was?'

'Dennis? Oh, he's having a drink somewhere.'

'Where is he, Tom?' insisted Sheila, suddenly realising there was more to it.

Before he could answer, the bus came in, emptied its trickle of passengers, and Tom and Sheila got on.

'Upstairs, Sheila. I could do with a smoke.'

She climbed the stairs and, out of the habit, went to sit at the front. They had the top deck to themselves.

'Right, Tom. What's this about being Dennis' alibi?'

'I don't suppose more dirt can make much difference now. He's been seeing somebody else, Sheila. And before you ask, I don't know who she is. We go into town together and meet later to come home and he leaves me like a lemon to either drink on my own or walk round the town,' explained Tom peevishly, 'and I think he's a swine doing this to you.'

She was looking out of the bus window, watching the streets of the town giving way to the countryside.

'And what are you doing to Rita?'

'She doesn't care where I am so long as I'm out of her way. And I've always thought a lot about you, so I suppose I was trying to teach him a lesson.'

By the time the bus reached the top of their road, they'd both fallen into their own thoughts.

'Are you coming in with me, Sheila?' invited Tom, almost pathetically.

Sheila crossed the road towards her own house. 'You must be joking, Tom. You look after *your* problems. I've got my own. Remember?'

Jacko

Barbara Stewart

REGULAR as clockwork, at hay-time and harvest, Jacko returned to the farm. A small man with shaggy hair and a wrinkled skin, his rough appearance was alleviated by his humorous grey eyes. He wore a torn dirty raincoat, intended for a stouter man. It was held together by a knotted leather strap; probably part of an obsolete leading rein. His disreputable boots were tied with ginger string which flapped rhythmically as he loped along. With a flat greasy cap perched on his head, he would stand at the back door of the farmhouse.

'Got any work, Missis?' he'd ask, touching his cap.

'Better ask the Boss,' Mrs Round invariably answered, 'but first I'll get you a bite to eat.' Then she bustled back to the kitchen table and put a slab of cheese between two thick slices of bread. Handing this over along with a pint pot of hot sweet tea, she'd tell him, 'They're over in the ten acre today, best get up there to see what's doing.'

She never asked Jacko indoors, even on bitterly cold days when the wind was swirling the wet straw up and around in mini-cyclones and the hail rapped a threatening tattoo on the corrugated iron roofs of the outhouses. She used to. Until the day he'd been and gone, and left a haze of fleas jumping up and down on the clippie rug in front of the great fireplace. She got rid of the musty odour by opening the back door for a while, but the fleas were more persistent. Since then, she'd kept him on the outside of the back door.

He slept in the straw in the loft above the stables and probably felt more at home with the shuffling, snorting horses for company than he would have done in a house.

When he worked, Jacko was a grafter. But there were periods when he didn't feel like work. Then he'd pack his bits and pieces in an old khaki haversack and return to the road.

It was a restlessness inside him which drove him on. On to new towns, through county after county, although always in the North, sleeping under hedges and behind hay-ricks. A day's work here or a week's there was sufficient to earn enough for his simple needs. When in work, he ate well, the farmer's wife saw to that, and when he was on the road, well, he scrounged a bit here and there or helped himself to a turnip or a capful of apples as he tramped the open road. He was a man of Spartan tastes, though he enjoyed a few pints, given the opportunity.

He was well known in York and Pannal where he worked the cattle markets. And, being willing and of a pleasant disposition, he was not often refused employment. So the day inevitably came when he knocked on Mrs Round's door.

'Got any work, Missus?' he asked. There was no humour in his grey eyes on this occasion. They were dull and lacklustre. His skin looked grey beneath the weather beaten tan and he swayed as he stood in the doorway.

'You're not well, Jacko,' exclaimed Mrs Round. 'Look, go straight round to the stables. I'll bring you a blanket and something to eat. You really should be living under a proper roof. You know, you could stay at the Lodge in Pontefract.'

'Nay, Missus, if it came to that, I'd rather be dead,' avowed Jacko. He turned and made his unsteady way across the stockyard.

Mrs Round warmed some soup on the stove and cut some chunks of bread. She mashed some strong tea and sweetened it heavily. With a blanket over her arm and a basket containing one jug of tea and another of soup, she went after Jacko.

'Thanks, Missus,' he said, 'You're good to me.'

He held the mug of tea between both hands and gulped the steaming liquid. Colour crept back into his face but it was more the flush of fever than of health.

'You should see a doctor.......' began Mrs Round.

He stopped her with a shake of the head.

'No doctors. Don't hold with 'em. A good night's sleep and I'll be as right as I want to be.'

Mrs Round left him then. No arguing with stubborn men. As she knew from a lifetime's experience.

'No arguing. No anything,' Farmer Round told his wife later that night when he returned from checking the patient in the stable. 'Jacko's had the last word.'

Deserving Case

Joan Thornton

'HASN'T he got a skinny bottom?' Ronnie turned abruptly and sat down, his face crimson.'Of course, he's not got much meat on him at all.' He slumped low, trying to disappear into the sagging cushions of the armchair.

The two ugly sisters - gross Granny Pollock and even grosser Great-aunty Edith, like Tweedledum and Tweedledee - sat on the facing sofa, passing indiscriminately offensive comments back and forth. 'And them baggy trousers they all wear these days make him look worse. But then he takes after his dad.' The accusation was emitted in a long derisory snort through Granny Pollock's horribly hairy nostrils.

Which inspired most disapproval, Ronnie wondered, his absentee father or his small arse? Probably both. How could so much fat tolerate such leanness? And his dad? Well, he'd left two years before: ipso fatso, according to Granny Pollock, it had to be his dad's fault. For one thing, the blubber with the mouthpiece was his mam's mam, and for another, she automatically disapproved of half the human race on the grounds of it being male and exploiters of the weaker sex. Then it was Ronnie's turn to snort in derision, but he covered the sound with his handkerchief and blew his nose. *Weaker sex!* Granny Pollock bore as much resemblance to the weaker sex as The Incredible Hulk.

With his dad gone, Ronnie'd done his best to be the man of the family and look after his mam and young Jimbo, but it was a heavy burden to carry at fourteen. A changeling, without distinction of being man or boy, he reaped the disadvantages of both and the benefits of neither.

'Ronnie, please.' His mam's half-pleading, half-whining voice penetrated his gloom. 'Aunty Edith wants another cup of tea so be a good lad and make another pot.'

'And if you've got a biscuit, please,' wheedled Aunty Edith. 'I'm starving. I've hardly eaten a thing all day.'

'Apart from half an ox, three sheep, five loaves and two

fishes,' thought Ronnie, glaring at the 'starving' figure. He looked away in case she saw the contempt in his eyes.

As he went out to the kitchen, Eric, the mangy old black and white tom who'd adopted them when they moved into the house, slunk through the doorway. Looking the worse for wear after a night on the tiles, he was seeking somewhere to lay his head, and probably off-load some fleas at the same time.

'Oooo's a bootiful pussy then?' invited Aunty Edith, trying to lure him onto her knee.

'Chichichichichi,' encouraged Granny Pollock, vying for his attention.

Eric made his choice and climbed, arthritically, into Aunty Edith's well upholstered lap.

'Aren't ooo a boooootiful kitty-witty.' She stroked him from head to tail as he circled her lap preparing to settle down for a nap. 'A lovely-wuvly pussy-wuss....' She interrupted herself midstream. 'Isn't he thin?' she declared indignantly. 'Does this cat get enough to eat? The poor thing's starving, I can feel all his backbone when I stroke him.'

Her obsession with food was only equalled by her obsession with cats and when the two coincided, she was unbearable. Ronnie closed the connecting door to cut out the sound of her voice, but it went through the wood like an electric saw.

'A chain saw,' reflected Ronnie, 'would shut her up nicely - and permanently.'

He made some fresh tea and carried the teapot and a packet of biscuits into the front room. He carefully poured another cup for Aunty Edith while she ripped open the packet and sank her fangs into a chocolate digestive. Two gulps, it was gone and she reached for another.

'....Well, you want to make sure he stays on at school. It'll make the best of what little he's got upstairs and at least he'll have the chance to make something of himself, instead of taking after his dad,' observed Aunty Edith, spraying crumbs as she stuffed another biscuit into the yawning cavern of her mouth.

Ronnie envisaged climbing in there and packing Semtex between the boulders of her molars. He pressed the plunger and blasted her head into oblivion, her evil spirit escaping from the stump of her neck like an erupting volcano, the noxious blast rising high and spreading on the air currents before descending to contaminate the world. Picturing the ending, he quickly revised it. Better that the forces of evil were trapped within the mountain. He set a smaller charge: enough to make her head collapse on itself and stop her mouth so the malignancy and corruption couldn't escape.

Why did his mam take so much crap from the vindictive old witches? They pried and poked, criticised and condemned; neither truth nor fact essential to their evil opinions. Experts in the art of character assassination, they homed in on physical or emotional failings like vultures to carrion.

'I'm sorry,' a patent lie, 'but you know me, I speak my mind.' Thus spoken, it was taken as clearance for delivering ungodly offence without further apology. It was amazing though how sensitive and quick to take umbrage they were if anybody dared respond with like.

'Granny Pollock has been good to us since your dad went, so show some gratitude,' mam reminded them regularly, especially when there was imminent danger of a visit. 'And Aunty Edith is Granny's sister, so try to be nice to her. We're all she's got.'

'And is there any friggin' wonder!' concurred Ronnie and Jimbo, safely out of earshot.

Jimbo had sloped off with the excuse of football practice when he heard they were turning up for tea; and no doubt he'd stay away till they were long gone. Ronnie seethed at Jimbo getting his excuse in first because when he said he wanted to do his homework over at his mate's house, he lost out. He'd dodged their last couple of visits so this time mam made no bones about expecting him to put in an appearance.

'Friggin' hell,' muttered Ronnie, unable to tune out the dynamic duo as they explained in tedious detail a recent excursion round local mill shops in search of bargain woollies in giant economy sizes - Euro-sizes, more likely. However, a change of subject brought no respite.

'....I don't know why you let him have his hair cut like that - all stuck up and spiky,' objected Aunty Edith. 'Crew cut it was called when we were young. The American air force wore it like that.'

Her lips curled in distaste as if recalling a disagreeable memory and Ronnie, knowing she'd been in the WAAF during the war, tried to imagine what kind of experiences might account for her aversion to his hairstyle. But her penetrating voice distracted him from the erotic and lewd images he tried to induce.

Like a tick on a dog, once she'd got her teeth in, she didn't let go till she'd drawn blood. 'He's too thin, you know!'

'According to her, the whole population's underweight,' mocked Ronnie silently, 'Less than five meals a day and you're undernourished. There's enough meat on the pair of them to feed half the third world.'

He pictured the pair of them: trussed and rotating on a spit till the fat splashed and sizzled in the fire underneath, rendering them down to the size of large, ugly monkeys. He'd read somewhere that badly burned bodies were reduced to about half their normal size. Black and shrivelled, with bones poking through shrunken flesh. Like the roast leg of lamb Granny Pollock put on the table when they'd gone round for Sunday dinner the weekend before.

'There must be something wrong with his diet or he wouldn't be so spotty,' pointed out Granny Pollock.

'There is *not!* It's his age.' His mam was indignant and Ronnie had the satisfaction of knowing they'd got up her nose at last, if only because of the insinuation that she neglected her sons. An uncomfortable silence followed but for the crunch of guzzled digestives.

The crackle of cellophane woke Piggy from his slumber. Dad had brought the stray dog from work where it had been scrounging round the dairy for a week or more and the manager was threatening to have it put down because of hygiene regulations. Initially christened Pete, it was soon evident that Piggy was an eating machine. The minute he'd bolted his own grub, he'd beg at the table so pitifully you could easily believe he hadn't eaten for a week. He'd also become disgustingly obese and waddled when he walked.

'That poor dog's starving,' complained Aunty Edith, in the process of devouring another chocolate digestive. 'See how he's looking at me. Give him a biscuit, he wants something to eat.'

'No,' said Ronnie firmly. 'He's on a diet, he's too fat.'

'He's not fat,' she denied indignantly, as if the accusation had been directed at herself. Her indignation turned to a simper, 'He's just pleasantly plump.'

Ronnie resented her freely dispensing the chocolate digestives. It was the last packet and there'd be no more till his mam did her weekly shop next Friday. Besides, they were wasted on Piggy who, Jimbo'd discovered in a recent taste test, couldn't differentiate between chocolate and a used tea bag - he scoffed them both.

'Look how he's watching me! Poor thing....' Piggy knew a sucker when he saw one. Aunty Edith broke her biscuit in half and offered it to him. It disappeared down his neck untasted and he waited eagerly for more.

Ronnie gritted his teeth. 'I'll move the tray if everybody's finished,' he offered, with the intention of preserving the rest of the biscuits from Aunty Edith's greedy eyes. He scooped the tray from the table just as her talons swooped down for another.

'Sorry,' he said loftily, in the way his mam did when what she actually meant was you've been warned so it serves you right, 'you shouldn't have given any to the dog.'

Ronnie marched into the kitchen, ignoring the gasps of outrage and surprise which followed him out. He deposited the tray on the drainer as he passed, lifted his jacket from the hook behind the back door and continued through, slamming it hard after him, so he wouldn't hear his mam shouting at him to come back and apologise.

He stomped out of the house and down the street, strode past the bus stop and turned left on the corner. No doubt he'd find some of his mates down at the the snooker hall. It was a couple of miles to town but the walk would give him time to calm down.

The steady drizzle gradually increased till the rain was coming down like rods, piercing his shower-proof jacket and Chinos. In no time, he was wet to the skin and his clothes clung heavy and uncomfortable, but he'd no intention of turning back. He walked faster and the effort generated heat. He could feel it building up, trapped inside his clothing.

When the canal came into sight, he turned away from the road, took the steps down the banking and headed towards the bridge. Even before he got there, his nose wrinkled in anticipation of the festering stink of urine, decomposing rubbish and stagnant water under the bridge. When he got closer, it was more pungent than he remembered and he spit in disgust, as if doing so would rid the stench from his nose.

Semi-inflated condoms swirled on the scummy surface of the canal, bringing to mind the erotic gyrations of a belly dancer. He smirked at the memory of Jimbo's obsessive interest in a recent TV documentary featuring one. His mam was bothered by what she considered an unhealthy interest in sex for a nine year old, and asked their dad to discuss the facts of life with Jimbo next time he visited. Only then was it revealed that his interest lay in the large ruby-coloured gem embedded in her navel and how she kept it in place.

Stimulated by thoughts of Rachel Padley, a girl in Ronnie's economics class who currently featured in many of his fantasies, he could only imagine the canal bridge as a dark, degrading place for young lovers to grope out their lust. He would never bring Rachel here and the thought revolted him almost as much as the place did. However, it offered shelter till the rain eased off. Unzipping his jacket, he wafted the fronts to circulate cool air round his steaming armpits. The wet fabric of his shirt chilled suddenly against his skin, he shuddered violently and quickly re-zipped his jacket before he lost too much heat.

He swung round suddenly at the sound of a scurry and a plop, as something unseen entered the water. 'A rat,' said

Ronnie aloud. 'Must be loads of rats round the canal.' The sound of his voice, intended to make the place seem less desolate, came back at him not as a clear echo but as a mocking undertone. He tried to control his imagination as it flicked through the pages of the worst horror stories he'd read: *The Rats, Lair, Domain....*

Another rustle in the shadows startled him briefly out of his daydream, giving him the chance to eject the gruesome fantasies. Instead, he shoved his fists deep into his pockets the better to protect fingers made vulnerable by James Herbert's images of razor-sharp, rodent incisors gnawing through bone.

It was time to move on. The drenching, cleansing rain held a certain allure. Half turning, he backed away from the canal edge and something rubbed against his ankle. With a startled yell, he lashed out his foot. Something soft and resisting, accompanied by a howl, hurled through the air and arched into the shadows. The shape declined into a splash. Ronnie ran.

He was well away from the bridge before he stopped to look back. Heart pounding, he half expected to be set upon and torn apart by a ravenous, hate-driven pack of monster rats. When he realised that nothing had followed him, he felt ridiculous and cowardly and thankful no-one was around to witness his gutless panic.

When his breathing slowed and the throbbing blood in his ears calmed, he picked up the noise of splashing and frantic miaows.

'Oh shit,' he said as his mind registered and identified the sounds. 'Only a cat, and I must have kicked it into the canal.'

He waited, his ears acute, hoping to hear it scramble onto the bank. The splashing continued but the miaows, to his ears, became more feeble. He pictured Eric in the cold, black water, too old and arthritic to struggle for long and knew he couldn't walk away and leave the poor beast to fend for itself.

Re-entering the shadow of the bridge, his eyes blindly scanned the surface of the water, taking time to readjust to the lack of light. Then he saw its head bobbing on the surface, the small mouth opening and closing but no longer crying. A floating plastic bottle bumped against its head and the cat disappeared for a moment, then surfaced again, wet and straggly and wretched.

Ronnie only intended entering that cold murky water as a last resort. He scanned around for something long enough to reach the cat and hook it out of the water. Some sort of pole, a branch. At the far side of the bridge something rigid stuck six inches out of the water. He raced off to investigate. A metal tube, a piece of discarded or vandalised scaffolding, looked as if it had been dumped over the bridge. It was near enough for him to reach and tug at it. It loosened and leaned. Ronnie grabbed, fearing it might disappear into the depths. He yanked, came perilously close to losing his balance, and the pole came out of the sucking mud.

He rushed back to the cat, afraid that the last of its lives had been accounted for, that it had disappeared for good under the water. It was still floundering weakly. But as he stretched the pole out, it seemed to understand that he was trying to help and a water-slicked paw tried to anchor its claws, unsuccessfully, into the smooth metal. Ronnie tried to hook the pole under the cat's belly and lift it. He almost managed it, the cat was partly out of the water when it slipped off the pole and slithered under the water again. Up it came, not ready to give up the struggle now it had a rescuer.

After two more abortive attempts, Ronnie realised the only way was to get the end of the pole under the cat's arms, or the feline equivalent, and trawl it to the water edge. Slowly, gently, he drew the soddened animal towards him.

'What are you doing, boy?'

The voice exploded under the bridge and resonated round him. He looked to his right and a squat, bulky shape silhouetted under the archway loomed towards him. His distraction caused the cat to slip off the pole again. Footsteps came nearer and the booming voice demanded to know what he was doing. Ronnie considered it quite obvious to anyone with half a brain, so he ignored the woman and concentrated on trying to reposition the pole.

'You leave that helpless creature alone, you mindless hooligan.'

An umbrella prodded him viciously in the small of his back, almost tumbling him head first into the canal. He lost control of the pole and accidentally hit the cat on the head. Not hard, but enough to make it go under again. The umbrella went for his kidney and painfully connected. He swung round to grab the umbrella point before it did any more damage, but she wrenched it from his grasp.

'Young... thug... mindless... vandal... wretched... moron... cat... murderer...' each word punctuated by a blow from the umbrella. She was smaller than him, but she carried some weight - and she was quick. Fending off blows that hailed round his head and shoulders, he tried to explain.

'Prison's... too good... the likes... of you... good... birching... thrash some... sense...'

He pointed to the canal. The cat was no longer to be seen in the water.

'Old ladies... not safe... your sort... loose... on the... street.'

Ronnie was incensed. While she was busy beating him up, the cat had drowned. Then the umbrella caught his ear and the excruciating pain felt like his ear had been ripped off.

An overwhelming surge of fury rushed over him with such force that, even if he'd tried, it would have swamped any attempt to resist it. He was charged with a violent, uncontrollable hatred, directed at Aunty Edith and Granny Pollock and all the loathsome, interfering, peevish old women like them who were indiscriminately prejudiced; against blacks, foreigners, homosexuals, heterosexuals, males, unmarried women, children, teenagers, poor people, rich people, thin people - everybody who didn't conform to their hateful, small-minded, miserly, soulless standards.

He tore the umbrella from her grasp and swung it with all his strength. She screeched in fear and outrage. It made him angrier. It confirmed his suspicions. She was of the same ilk, dispensing punishment, expecting no retaliation.

He lashed at her with the umbrella again and again; for the drowned cat, for his mam, for his dad, for Jimbo, for all persecuted and intimidated people, but most of all for himself. Again and again and again. Till his fury was spent.

He looked at the limp bundle by his feet. There was some blood on her face, not much. She was very still. She didn't seem to be breathing but he didn't check too closely. Scanning the surface of the canal for any sign of the cat, seeing none, he dropped the umbrella into the water and watched it sink slowly as the air, trapped in the nylon folds, glubbed out.

Indifferent to the rain, Ronnie climbed the steps to the road. He paused at the top and looked up and down the street. There was nobody in sight so he continued in the direction of the snooker hall.

'Some old women deserve to be mugged,' he muttered defensively. 'In fact, mug 'em all. Mug 'em all.'

He repeated it over and over in his mind till it slipped into the tune of *Bless 'Em All*. Then the rain suddenly came down harder than ever and, appropriately, he switched to singing *When You Walk Through A Storm*.

It reminded him that the cup final was only a few weeks away. He had a ticket and a coach-load from school were going down for the match. The thought cheered him and he hurried towards the snooker hall.

The Seeds of Destruction

Les Adlington

IN MAY 1947 old Hubert Goodall sent a wrecking crew from the brewery to demolish the Low Drop of the once prestigious Montrose Arms. The Low Drop had for the past thirty years been ruled with bare-fisted truculence by bartender Anthracite Abe McBean, former heavyweight champion of Great Britain and the Empire. This was the start of an inexorable decline for the town of Minesbrough in South Yorkshire.

Even as the Low Drop was going under the breakers' hammer, the aesthetic fabric of the old town was under siege only yards away on the Bottom Road. The demise of Minesbrough's historic Tuxford Picture Palace, however, came about following a bizarre sequence of events and could hardly claim to be victim of post-war austerity or even of the changing nature of English life. In fact, the closure of the Tuxford could be planted firmly at the flat, wellingtoned feet of luckless Ronnie Bonney, a citizen of pathetic prominence from nearby Sowton.

This inept little man owed his notoriety to a squat stature, a fat rotundity, a hairless head concealed under a perennial flat cap, a patent shortage of grey matter and a squeaky voice - the latter his one defence against generations of marauding school children who sought him out relentlessly. In that momentous year of 1947 when Ronnie Bonney was 47 years old, he looked no different to what he had looked in 1927 and for that matter, what he still looked in 1967 when he joined his beloved *Riders In The Sky.*

He lived with his elder brother, a Sowton dignitary rumoured to have inherited Ronnie's share of the family brains, though this could never be verified. Strangely for one so docile and dilatory, Ronnie Bonney was always in work and each week he handed over to his brother the whole of his pay packet in return for a roof over his head. The only exception was the few coppers it took to get him into the cheapest seats at a nightly picture show, with a quarter of Poor Bens for sustenance.

During the war years, when Ronnie was employed at the Pinehurst Sewage Works, he was obliged to catch the same bus home as colliers from the local pit. Few colliers, however, were prepared to board should Ronnie be spotted in his favourite front seat. The stench was unbearable on his worst days and hardly tolerable on his best. Had it not been for his brother's political muscle, the Minesbrough & Sowton Traction Company would certainly have banished Ronnie from all services. As it was, the conductress was issued with tongs and gasmask to collect his fare. In a desperate bid to counteract the legacy of his brief but potent journey, doors and windows remained open whatever the weather long after Ronnie had alighted at his Sowton stop.

The older Bonney, from his pedestal of civic power, attempted to use his authority to protect poor Ronnie from the worst of his tribulations. While this worked quite well in certain areas like the workplace (where pressure could be applied to management to watch out for Ronnie's welfare) it proved useless in the face of the local juvenile population.

Given Ronnie's child-like mentality and love of the cinema, the Tuxford Picture Palace in Minesbrough was an obvious alternative when he was hounded out of his usual haunt at Sowton. But it was a decision which set that charismatic venue on a countdown to disaster.

The Tuxford had been for years a fertile quagmire in which thrived the worst manifestations of juvenile depravity. Though not every child who cut his teeth at the Tuppenny Rush on Saturday afternoons developed into a Buck Ruxton or John George Haigh, the Tuxford was not the place to nurture prospective saints. Even the most gentle characters were transformed into raving psychopaths once inside the famous batwing doors, clutching armfuls of rotting vegetables from nearby market stalls.

Now the Tuxford Picture Palace followed the classic design of seat arrangement in which plank seating stretched from one side of the cinema to the other with no central gangway, unlike the more expensive tip-ups behind and above. When Ronnie Bonney came to the Tuxford, he pitched camp in his preferred location - on the front planking, dead centre. Naturally in this situation, the provocative silhouette of Ronnie Bonney represented an irresistible target in front of the screen.

Children soon learned to leave a swathe of empty seats in Ronnie's catchment area so that the barrage of choice organic matter could home in on Ronnie's fat neck with little fear of offending the rest of the plank-bound audience. How Ronnie Bonney managed to survive these nightly shellackings from all manner of vegetable fallout speaks volumes for his total involvement in the filmshow. He missed not a flicker from curtain-up to the National Anthem through both houses, despite a persistent assault from the rear.

'Donkey muck!' howled the kids as endless volleys of rotten fruit and veg rained down on Ronnie's prominent profile.

'Ah'll tell our kid!' bawled Ronnie, still urging Buck Jones to keep his head down while the bandits passed.

All in all, Ronnie's row was a hard one to hoe and never more so than at the pictures he loved so dearly. But Ronnie was a man of marvellous resilience and fortitude. No lesser being could shrug off such daily torment. At the rush for the doors at the end of each night, Ronnie would shuffle outside with a cherubic beam of internal joy on his round, pink face.

For the best part of its life, the Tuxford had catered for an audience demanding blood and guts in unlimited quantities. A diet of Westerns had fed this bloodlust with ample fodder. It is however worthy of note   that   the quality of its crowds declined in direct proportion to the banality of its films.

While its reputation ensured that the more orderly Minesbrough elements steered clear of the Tuxford environs, unfortunately it served to periodically attract a disruptive influx from the adjacent mining community of Deane Abbey. It was this latter event, and a rejected load of decomposing pomegranates in the hands of the worst barbarians since Attila's Huns, which irrevocably tilted the scales against the Tuxford's survival - and after only five nights of Ronnie Bonney's fat backside occupying centre front on the planking.

Grasping owner Howard MacFadden contributed to his

misfortune. He chose the week of Bonney's debut to introduce a scheme of singular insanity. Belatedly, he decided to bring good taste and refined viewing to the Bottom Road. He booked in a high-budget John Wayne feature 'Flame of the Barbary Coast' at the expense of such trusted stalwarts as Tom Mix and Charles Starrett. The rabble were not impressed.

Saturday night crowds contained the most disquieting segments of Minesbrough society. It was their night and they made it a rough one. On this particular Saturday, circumstances combined to ensure the fall of a great institution.

As Ronnie Bonney took up his usual seat clutching his ration of Poor Bens, so the lawless Minesbrough hard-core massed at the rear. When the lights faded, a Deane Abbey contingent of tough eggs - who'd not wanted to be seen entering the cheapest seats - slipped in alongside Ronnie Bonney, under cover of darkness, oblivious to the inherent danger.

It began the minute John Wayne appeared on screen dressed not in cowboy gear, but in a namby-pamby Victorian 3-piece suit including flowered silk waistcoat and string tie. The catcalls erupted immediately and the first cascades of rotten fruit descended around Ronnie Bonney's plump neck, incorporating the new technology of the soggy pomegranate. As these potent missiles thudded into Ronnie's bulging back and shoulders, a rainbow of scattershot enveloped the unsuspecting Deane Abbey posse.

The sense of outrage emanating from their violated ranks came as a complete surprise to the assailants in the rear. Had the presence of Deane Abbey troops been suspected, there would have been no assault at all. But Ronnie Bonney's fat head had been the target and little attention had been devoted to minor details. War, as a matter of course, ensued.

Owner Howard MacFadden, witness to frequent affrays, recognised the extraordinary virulence of this particular outbreak. He switched off the projector and turned on the lights. The Minesbrough force on the higher ground gasped audibly at the unnerving sight of Deane Abbey infantry running amok. Saturday night garb of spattered suits, splotched ties, sodden suede shoes and the latest hairstyles dripping pomegranate seeds were sights to chill the blood.

Screaming like Mescalero Apaches, the Abbey boys retaliated with the weapons to hand, Howard MacFadden's period cinema furnishings. Planks were ripped out and sent into the upper ranks. The Edwardian splendour of the Tuxford Picture Palace began to disintegrate. Fruit salvos rained down on the besieged few, bringing the screen down under a coating of pomegranate seeds. Howard MacFadden ran from the auditorium sobbing and shrieking for police assistance.

Flora Storey, the Tuxford's beguiling usherette, hoisted her skirts around her hips in a futile attempt to capture the attention of the warring factions. For the first time in her twenty years in charge of the famous Tuxford flashlight (which doubled as a truncheon in less harrowing skirmishes,) Flora Storey found her ample charms unequal to the task.

Stick by brick, the Tuxford's sumptuous squalor crumbled beneath the avalanche of pomegranate starshells and the ingenuity of the defending dismantlers. Ronnie Bonney picked seeds from his bag of Poor Bens and crouched lower under the creaking stage where he'd taken refuge. In the auditorium, eyes clogged, nostrils blocked and throats choked on pomegranate particles. The battle raged on as crowds gathered on the Bottom Road to witness the end of an era.

When the dust had settled on this disgraceful affair, Howard MacFadden and his step-daughter Trowell were noted one morning plastering huge notices either side of the legendary batwing doors: CLOSED FOR SUMMER PERIOD AND REFURBISHMENT

'Who's in that?' demanded Clarrie Muldoon, in passing.

'It's not a picture,' replied Trowell sadly, 'it's a travesty.'

'Nivver catch on 'ere, them travesties,' growled Clarrie.

'You see, my dear, what I've had to battle against all my life?' sighed Howard MacFadden. 'Trying to bring some meaning into the pitiful lives of these Minesbrough people. And what for?'

'Oh, come on, Dad,' said Trowell. 'In years to come, when they speak of the great days of the Tuxford Picture Palace, whose name will they remember?'

'Ronnie Bonney,' snarled Howard MacFadden.

Charlie

Tony Lumb

BILLY Brown was a bully. He would never alter. He would have to be put in his place before very long.

I was only saying to Charlie the other day: 'Why does he always pick on me?' But I knew the answer to that as well as Charlie did.

Billy was not so much a physical bully, although he could fetch you a lovely thick ear if the mood took him; no, he was more subtle than that. Like most of his kind, his targets were always smaller, younger and wore glasses or stuttered and were shy. All of these defects fitted me.

After an eye test at school, they found that I was short sighted and sent me to Castleford for some glasses. How terrible they looked. Thick glass lenses surrounded by tortoise-shell frames which made your ears go green.

It was six or seven weeks before I ventured outside without taking off my specs and the first time I did, who did I meet? You've guessed it - Billy Brown.

'What you doing with that bike on your face?' were his first words, 'You could get two rides on Gilligan's roundabout with them jam-jar bottoms,' he went on. My mates suddenly became *his* mates, laughing because it was expected of them.

'You know what's coming next,' I whispered to Charlie, 'I'm now going to be stuck with specky four eyes.'

Charlie nodded but they couldn't see him nod. In fact, they couldn't see Charlie at all, only I could see him or talk to him. Charlie was my best mate. He'd never laugh at me.

'Come on then, specky four eyes,' jeered Billy, as expected, 'Fetch thi bat and ball, let's have a game at cricket.' He went to find a dustbin for wickets and shouted over his shoulder: 'And I'm Denis Compton.'

Billy wasn't always bad, just nasty when he was. He'd play a good game of cricket or kick-out-can for a while until some rule wasn't to his liking. He was never out 'leg before' and here he was again, caught right in front of the wickets.

'Never!' he yelled, as we all appealed. I excitedly tried to tell him to 'come on and play fair Billy', but only came out with a rat-a-tat of c's and p's and b's.

'Shut thi gob and give thi arse a chance, Specky,' he sneered, knowing he'd get another laugh. 'What would you say if you could talk?' He threw the bat down, kicked the dustbin over and went for his tea.

Nobody seemed interested in cricket any more, so I picked up my bat and me and Charlie sauntered off home.

'I'll have him one day,' I said to Charlie, 'One of these days, I'll bloody have him.' Charlie agreed with me. He always did. Funny thing, I never stuttered when I talked with Charlie, maybe that's why he never laughed at me.

Like all bullies, Billy wasn't too smart. Me and Charlie could do him whenever we wanted to but we never let on that we could. It was pleasure enough to get one up on him. When the conker season came round, Billy would get out his niner. He reckoned he'd had it soaking in vinegar for two years and it had nine kills, more than any other in the backs. I played him one day with the old trick of a metal nut tied to the other end of the string and, with a bit of sleight of hand, I smashed his niner with my first hit. Billy never knew. He couldn't say much because there was a good crowd around and nobody else twigged it either. If they had, some sneak would have told Billy. Me and Charlie had a good laugh about that.

I could always beat him at marbles as well. I said it was because I could see better wearing glasses.

'Well, tha better take 'em off then and give us all a chance,'he quipped. He was in one of his better moods; he could have pinched some of my nigs. I used to let him win sometimes or he wouldn't have played any more. Charlie always knew when I'd let Billy win.

I could get at Billy in many crafty little ways but, since he didn't know I'd conned him, only me and Charlie could have a laugh. Billy often caught me grinning at Charlie, and he'd say: 'Hey, Milky Bar Kid, what you grinning at now? You're as daft as you look.'

My auntie May had a fish shop at the end of our street

and I could go in any time for some free chips. Billy knew, as did all the other kids, and on opening nights, Billy was very friendly.

'I could eat some chips,' Billy would say, obviously hinting at me. 'I'm real starving.'

I'd toddle off to the fish shop and come back with a bag of steaming chips. Billy didn't want to steal my chips in front of all his pals, so he used to tell a story for a chip.

'Once upon a time there were three bears....' That was as far as he got with all his stories. It was worth a chip to Billy. Soon he'd have had them all. Little did Billy know that when I came out of the shop, I'd sprinkled muck all over the chips. He couldn't tell the muck from the scraps. No wonder Charlie grinned as I went for some more.

Billy got worse. He had made more kids cry than anybody I know. Nobody liked him, not even his couple of cronies, he hated them as well. He forced himself on to everything that was going off. There was no doubt he would have to go.

The nights began to darken and get colder and we were soon into December. Christmas was coming. Our football season was over: Billy had booted my ball into someone's yard and they had kept it, so no soccer. We couldn't even have a game of cowboys without Billy turning up and spoiling the game. He was always the baddie and when he tied you up with the clothes line, you stayed tied up.

Just before Christmas, it snowed. It snowed for two days and we had a lovely covering for our Christmas games. Out came the sledges, or, if you hadn't one, you'd try to get dad to make you one. Our favourite place was up the muck stacks. We could be mountaineers climbing Everest or Scott of the Antarctic with our sticks and clothes lines.

Lots of kids were gathering on the stacks for the annual dare. Sledges came in all shapes and sizes from a piece of tin from an Anderson shelter to a proper home-made job with steel runners. Soon there were two or three slide paths down the stack which got nearer and nearer to the top. The big dare was the first lad to sledge down right from the top. It wasn't easy, that is it took a lot of courage. It was about fifty yards down to the bottom and there was a row of houses along the bottom with one small gap through. You had to hit this gap to take the steam out of your speeding sledge. It took a few hours of short runs to form the final run in and then came the dares. All the big lads daring each other, each one scared to death, but building up courage.

Billy was there with his heavy home-made sledge, sitting at the top a few yards to the right of the path with all the other would-be heroes. There was quite a crowd as me and Charlie walked up. Billy saw me. He was really scared, I could see it in his face. He broke the tension.

'Lend's thi glasses, Specky,' he shouted, hoping for a laugh to boost his flagging confidence, 'I want to see where I'm going.' Me and Charlie were right beside Billy now and he was flashily running his sledge backwards and forwards over the edge. All it would need, I thought, was one small push with my foot at the right time and Billy would be the first to go. I turned to go to the back of the crowd, when a shout went up.

'Billy's gone!' someone yelled.

I looked back over the edge. Billy had gone all right, but not on the right path. He was gathering speed at a tremendous rate and heading for the second house in the row. Billy wasn't smart enough to jump off into the snow. He just stared straight ahead, frozen to his sledge. It seemed like a slow motion dream, Billy desperately grasping the top of his sledge, his knuckles as white as the snow.

It was a perfect run. Everyone was silent. The only sound was the swish of Billy's sledge runners.

The dream came to an end when the sledge hit the house. The sledge stopped dead, but Billy didn't. His head hit the windowsill with a sickening thud. The white snow was splattered with Billy's blood and brains. Billy was dead.

Slowly, the kids started down the stack to look at Billy, leaving me and Charlie standing alone at the top.

'Billy's day has come at last, Charlie,' I said, 'I wonder why he went down there? It wasn't me that helped him on his way.'

I looked round at Charlie. He was grinning.

Noreen

James Goff

'BRAZEN hussy's expecting again.' Relaxing the pedal, Noreen Baines twisted the material beneath the needle before looking across the table. 'Keeps the hospital going on her own, that woman.'

Two snake-like threads ran out from the machine as her companion leaned back. With hands and teeth, she broke the cotton, snipped the ends, and tossed the garment onto the table between them. 'Got five already, hasn't she?' Her cropped auburn head, flecked with grey, tilted sideways as she altered the settings.

'Five?' Noreen cackled, displaying yellow teeth that wiggled up and down. 'You're out of touch, Ada Robshaw. Six, and not a pair of shoes between them. She'll be wore out by forty, and him six feet under.'

'My old man couldn't manage that,' Ada confessed. 'Spends all his time up the allotment and down the pub. Comes home when he's hungry.'

'Aren't you the lucky one? Last week I were stood at sink washing his vests. Up he comes behind me, great chest heaving, and snorting like a bullock. Chased me up the stairs, Ada. And what happened? The big Jessie tripped over the rug and skewered himself on the bedpost. Made his eyes water, I can tell you.'

'Should keep him quiet for a bit.' The voice was muffled as Ada rummaged in a box on her right.

'Morning, Mrs Robshaw.'

'God save us, Millie Arkwright, you gave me a turn! Get some strong boots, then we can hear you coming.'

'Looking perky this morning, lass. Been seeing your young man again?'

'Not this week, Mrs Baines. He's on twelve-hour shifts in the wash-house.' Leaning over, Millie scooped an armful of shirts, her ample bosom momentarily blocking the light that filtered through a dust-covered window.

'Look out! It's Frankenstein.' Noreen declared in a

hoarse whisper.

Millie straightened, turned, and collided with a brown-coated figure. 'Beg pardon, Mister Oldroyd.'

'All right, my dear. No harm done.' There was a sharp intake of breath as his eyes dropped from her face and paused. 'When you've pressed these, come and see me in the office.'

'Yes, Mister Oldroyd.' Swerving round him, Millie strode off, cheeks a delicate pink.

With the eyes of both women upon him, Oldroyd cleared his throat. 'Quiet in this corner, ladies. Run out of work?'

'Number six cotton, Frank. It keeps breaking. Always used number one when your father was living. It were a sorry day when he fell down the delivery shaft,' Noreen lamented, shaking her head.

'An order for five hundred from the Infirmary. If you feel you can't cope, perhaps it's time for someone younger.'

'Don't you threaten me, Frank Oldroyd. I remember you running round with cardboard shoes and no seat in your pants.'

A spluttering sound made them look at Ada. Head down, she was lining up two pieces of material. With a sniff, Oldroyd walked away, hands thrust deep into his pockets.

The chattering machines curtailed further conversation until a persistent clanging signalled the break for lunch. Noreen and Ada crossed the work-room slowly, bags in hand.

'Off to the cloakroom Noreen?'

'I allowed you more sense than that, Ada Robshaw. Full of dust, mice, sweaty feet, stale beer and cheap scent. Fresh air in the graveyard's too late for anybody. We'll eat outside, in God's canteen.'

Drawing back the bolts, Noreen heaved open the heavy door which led onto the fire escape. Soon they were sat on the cold iron steps, unwrapping sandwiches in the shade cast by the towering, smoke-blackened chimney nearby. Far below, ant-like figures scuttled about. Voices faint and without words drifted upward. Sandwich in one hand, flask top in the other, Ada looked over the rail and then skywards.

'Half way to Heaven, Noreen. Near as we'll ever get.'

'I'll come back and haunt this place when I'm gone, Ada.' Draining her cup, Noreen licked a finger and smacked her lips. 'Spent half me life here. And what for? Cheese and pickle sandwiches and coffee laced with rum.' Noreen rose slowly as the bell went.

'Getting on a bit, Ada. I'll not see twenty-five again.' As the door closed behind them, she stopped. 'That's Millie over there, coming out from Frankenstein's office.'

As they approached, Millie spotted them and altered course.

'Something's wrong, Noreen. Think she's been sacked?'

'By him? Course not. If there's any sacking, he should start with himself, great useless article. Millie! Over here, love.'

Threading her way between the machines, she stood before them, peering nervously over her shoulder.

'What's been going off, then?'

'I'm behind with me work, Mrs Baines.'

'And your hand? It's all grazed. What happened?'

'Suppose I caught it on something. Can't remember. I must go.' Millie retreated and pressed a switch. With a hiss of steam, the press opened and jerked into position.

'She's not saying, Noreen. It's a mystery.'

'Mystery my foot! He's tried it on and she's clocked him.'

'He wouldn't have the nerve. You're talking daft.'

The subject was closed and production resumed except for occasional glances in Millie's direction.

The office door opened. Frank approached, head down, stopping by their table.

'Number one cotton.' His voice was subdued and flat. Discoloration showed above and below his right eye, and his cheeks glowed hotly as Noreen met his gaze. Turning, he marched, head held high, back into the office.

'Daft, am I?' Noreen's eyes twinkled across the table to Ada. Her mouth twitched. She chuckled and Ada sniggered. They both leaned back and laughed.

The Greening of Crusoe Wilkins

Margaret Newton

THE black limousine purred to a halt outside 47 Mandela Way. The immediate family of the late Crusoe Wilkins strode up the short path and entered the house. Net curtains dropped into place. The show was over.

My mother rammed her hat on a coat peg, put on a flowered apron and went into the kitchen. 'Thank God that's over. I loved my father dearly, but I should never have agreed to that fiasco. It was the worst funeral I've ever been to.'

'I thought it was fun.' It was my first so I couldn't really say.

'Fun! Fun! You don't go to funerals to have fun.'

'Don't upset yourself, Amelia,' said Aunt Maud, 'It wasn't your fault Crusoe went a bit touched at the end.'

My mother rounded on her sister-in-law. 'I'll thank you not to slander my father like that. He may have been a bit eccentric but he wasn't daft.'

'Well, what would you call going ecological at his age?'

Aunt Maud had a point. Some people find God in old age. Grandad discovered the Greens and at eighty-four decided to do his bit to save the world.

'We should be proud of him,' said my father, 'trying new ideas at his age.'

'Trust you to stick up for him,' Mother snapped.

Sloughing off the role of peacemaker, he went into the front room and handed round plates of boiled ham to the waiting guests. My mother slammed a cupboard door.

'Do you want any help?' I offered.

'Haven't you helped enough? You and the BBC have a lot to answer for.' She burst into tears and ran upstairs.

She wasn't being fair. All I'd done was visit Grandad while he was watching Panorama. It was about the hole in the ozone layer and he asked me what I thought. I'd joined the Young Greens and gone veggie so we had a great discussion.

'Yorkshire folk used to be green,' he said. 'In the old days we always put horse muck on the rhubarb.'

I took him some leaflets and maybe they helped convince

him. The first my mother heard about it was when we called round to his house with his clean washing.

'I hope this lot's not full of phosphates?' he said, inspecting his pyjamas for left-on stains.

'I've done them in White Out, same as always,' said mother, 'so let that be an end of it.'

But that wasn't the end. The home help phoned to say that he was being difficult over her aerosol air freshener. She was a real treasure, so my mother went round. He was happily cutting up the Radio Times into little squares to recycle as loo paper. Of course, they blocked the toilet and after the third call-out the plumber suggested that Grandad was put in a home.

I'd always admired Grandad. He'd been a sailor, and the entire sixteen years I'd known him, he'd had a wooden peg leg. He'd been offered a modern leg but refused. The peg enhanced his sailor image. I asked him how he'd lost it.

'Fighting for King and Country.'

'Rubbish,' said my mother, 'he fell down the trap door at the pub fighting over a woman.'

When his old wooden leg split, he didn't want to use more endangered hard wood, so decided to try an aluminium one instead. The physios did their best but he never really got on with it. So when the scouts appealed for drinks cans, he sent them his new leg and repaired his old wooden peg with sticking plaster.

When my mother recovered from her hysterics and rejoined the wake, the cousins were eager to hear her side.

'Lovely do, Amelia,' they soothed. 'It was a blessed release. You've put up with a lot.'

'You don't know the half of it.'

'We can imagine. Still, it's all over now bar the shouting.'

'It's the shouting I'm worried about. It's bound to be in the Yorkshire Post. And I can just see the headline - PENSIONER BURIED IN CARDBOARD BOX.

'People might not have noticed.'

'Of course they noticed. It had KEEP THIS WAY UP stamped on it. We might have been able to disguise it with flowers, but covered in organic veg - no chance.'

'I didn't know where to look when the cabbage hit the vicar's ankle,' smirked Aunt Maud.

The vicar had been upset by the funeral arrangements. Singing 'All things bright and beautiful,' was one thing, but grandad had left instructions to plant organic veg on his plot and sell the resulting produce for church funds. The vicar only agreed because the church needed a green image. After the burial though, the vicar had thrown his green wellies behind a yew tree and gone to the pub with the funeral director who'd also had a difficult day. He'd had to pay extra handling charge to the men. Not being made to measure, they'd had to pack the box with bin liners and bind it up with insulating tape.

'It gives a bad impression, bundling the elderly off in such a penny pinching manner,' complained the funeral director.

The vicar agreed. He'd had a summons from his Bishop.

I should never have gone with Grandad to Comet. He'd headed straight to the freezer section. He arranged to have the freezer delivered to our house and the carton to his own address. In the taxi going home he gave a contented sigh.

'Right, that's settled.'

'What've you just done?'

'Bought me coffin.'

'He's done what?' shouted my mother. `He can't.'

But he could. She only got the new freezer if she agreed.

'It's cheap, biodegradable and not hurting trees. Oaks should be left where they belong, standing in a forest.'

Bemused relatives gradually drifted away. We cleared away the half-eaten debris. Grandad had gone, and with all the fuss we'd had no time to grieve. I felt sad but proud.

'Do you think he was right?' my mother asked that night.

'Yes. Perhaps he went a bit too far though. He sort of got carried away by it all in the end.'

But grandad had certainly made his point. The local paper ran a series of articles on green issues and the council set up a bottle and waste paper bank. It was called the CRUSOE WILKINS COLLECTION POINT. It was only right. They owed him public recognition, for it was under one of their refuse carts that he fell to his death when his peg leg finally broke completely in two.

Double Sixteen

Julian Bharier

JIM, the elderly landlord at the Yoredale Arms, hobbled arthritically around the bar to throw a small, weathered elm log on the fire. He gave it a desultory prod with a short brass poker. With one huge knarled hand, he picked up four empty straight pint glasses from a copper-topped table; with the other, he gave the table a quick wipe with a damp dishcloth pulled from his pocket.

'Quiet tonight,' he muttered, to no-one in particular.

'Ay,' agreed Lol, the only other customer, sitting on his usual stool at the end of the bar so he could lean against the wall, 'Quiet.'

'Ay. Allus is when t'team's away,' Jim explained.

'You don't play darts, then?' I asked Lol tentatively. In the few weeks since I moved to the village, I hadn't spent much time in the pub: an occasional quick pint after an evening's decorating and, if the mood took me, a slower one at mid-day on Sunday. I was on nodding terms only with the locals and had not previously spoken with Lol, who appeared to be a permanent fixture on the end stool.

'Used to,' said Lol slowly, looking straight ahead, once he had taken a swallow of Carlsberg.

'Used to be one of t' best in t'Dales,' said Jim, hobbling back behind his counter, 'Weren't many could beat Lol.'

'Ay, used to,' repeated Lol, draining the last inch of his Danish lager and putting his straight pint glass on the bar.

'Can I get you one?' I volunteered. He swivelled slowly on his stool until his eyes met mine. They narrowed as his craggy features crinkled into a slight smile.

'Ay, that's right kind of you,' he said, with a hint of surprise in his voice. Jim pulled two pints, a lager for Lol and a John Smith's for me. 'All the best, young man.'

'All the best,' I replied, 'So what made you give it up?'

'Eh?'

'The darts.'

'Oh.' Lol turned back ponderously to face the bar. He

took two lengthy sips of lager. 'Jim knows, don't you, Jim?'

'Ay, I know alreet,' said Jim, rinsing out his dishcloth. Neither seemed to consider that there was any more to be said. I took a couple of swallows and put my glass on the dark-wood bar in front of the china pump-handles.

'Ay,' I said, unable to come up with the key to keep the conversation alive. Jim started rinsing dirty glasses. Lol just stared into his lager. I turned to look at the fire. The flames cast shadowy patterns on the dark oak beams in the small bar-room and sought out reflections in the plates, cups and horse brasses on the walls. Lucky that the only pub in the village was a real pub, I thought: no piped music, no one-armed bandits, no imitation panelling, no childish jokes on notice boards. Even the cigarette machine was out of sight in the entrance hall, next to a row of coat hooks, not interfering with the pub's warm and homely, if slightly shabby, atmosphere.

'Ay,' said Lol suddenly, still surveying his glass. 'It was all an accident.'

'An accident?'

'Ay. It was nearly five years ago now. That's right, isn't it, Jim?'

'Ay. Would be near five year.'

'It was in this very place.'

'Ay.'

'And 'twas not my fault.'

'Nay. No-one were to blame.'

'I've never played since.'

'Not a single game. Not even for fun.'

'It was no fun on that night.'

'Nay. 'Twere no fun at all.'

Lol sipped some lager. Jim inverted the glasses on a bar towel to let the soapsuds drain off. I drank some bitter. Lol sipped again. Only the crackling of the log fire broke the minutes of silence before he continued.

'It was the semi-final of the Dales Cup,' he said in his gentle, deliberate North Yorkshire brogue, 'We were agin the King's Head.'

'Ay. Kings's Head.'

'There was a good crowd. Nigh on thirty, I'd think.'

'At least thirty. All cheering us on.'

'It was close, that match. By! It was close. Four all. Johnny Bell should've won and didn't, and George Thwaite, who hardly ever wins, had some real luck. The rest went as expected. It all came down to me against Big Arthur of the Head. And that was close too.'

'Ay. Nowt in it. And because it were t'decider, you had to play best of three and it were one all, weren't it?'

'Ay. One all and very even in t'third. But Big Arthur just slipped a little and I managed to get ahead. Left myself with two arrows and a double sixteen to win. One of the easiest doubles on the board.'

'The easiest.'

'You're right there, Jim. The easiest. But it's the story of my life. Every time things were looking bright, someone put the shutters up. Every time I had a chance to race ahead, someone put an obstacle in t'way.'

'Someone or summat.'

'Ay, that's right, Jim. Shouldn't say someone.   If it wasn't plain bad luck, it was probably written in my book up there. Nay, I shouldn't blame anyone else. That's not fair.' He sipped his lager at length. 'Nay. That's not fair.'

'Double sixteen, eh?' I murmured, to preserve the momentum.

'Ay. Double sixteen. And the crowd knew it was an easy one. Got up from their chairs and stools and pressed around. Shouted encouragement, then went quiet as I took extra careful aim. When that arrow left my hand, it felt like a winner. Sometimes you can tell, you know. Sometimes it just feels right.'

'Ay. Looked like a winner all t'way.'

'But it wasn't, was it? It hit the wire on the corner of the double sixteen. But instead of glancing past into the board or dropping to the floor, it ricocheted. Before you could shout a warning, it flew straight into the eye of Amy Brown. You don't know Amy. She was one of the prettiest little lasses in the village. Still is pretty, I'll warrant, except for that eye she lost. She's married now; lives somewhere in

Wales. I'll never forget the sight of that eye as long as I live.'

'She were lucky it didn't kill her.'

'Ay. It was a real mess. She didn't scream or cry much. Took it very calmly. The shock, I suppose. Everyone was helpful. Someone found a bandage and one of the locals, can't remember who, took her to t'Dales Hospital. I was probably more upset than she was. Said right there and then I was never going to play another darts match as long as I lived. Still had the one arrow left but I wouldn't throw it. Gave the match to Big Arthur and the King's Head went to the final. Didn't do them much good, though. They lost badly to the Rose and Crown. Any road, I've not thrown a dart since that night.'

'It must have been a nasty experience.'

'Ay. For me and for a lot who were here.'

'I'll never forget it, that's for sure,' said Jim, 'It were not like owt I've seen in any of t'pubs I've owned.'

Lol drank the last of his lager and I finished my bitter. He insisted it was his round. I hadn't intended to drink more than two pints that evening. But I accepted the offer; it would have been churlish not to.

'Cheers,' I said, raising my newly-filled glass to Lol and feeling just a little light-headed, 'You know what they say about car accidents. You should always get back in the car and drive again as soon as possible. Maybe that's what you should have done - thrown some more darts right away to get the accident out of your system.'

'Ay, but this was different. I'd never hurt anyone in my life and I'd be frightened to do it again. It could be worse next time. Nay, it was written in my book. No more darts matches for Lol.'

'But the chances of an accident like that happening again are very remote, surely?'

'I've never seen t'like of it before or since,' agreed Jim.

'And,' I said, 'I bet you could still hit that double sixteen with one dart even after all this time.'

'Ay. Happen I could. But I'm not going to.'

'Go on, Lol,' urged Jim. 'There's none but us here and we'll stand well out of t'way. It can't hurt.'

'Nay. I'll break my promise to myself. It's not meant to be.'

'Nay, Lol. You promised yourself not to play another match. This'd be but one arrer. Show the lad here how good you were.' Lol stared uneasily into his glass. I didn't want to press the matter, but Jim was becoming unnecessarily insistent. 'Give it a go, Lol. Just t'one.'

'Nay. I'm not sure.' He looked at me; I shrugged, beginning to wish I had not become involved. Then he looked at Jim, who was already taking a pack of darts out of a small cupboard behind the bar. 'Oh, all right. But be it on your head, Jim. Give me an arrow. I threw my set away after that terrible night. Threw them right in that fire over there. Never wanted to see another dart as long as I lived.'

Lol slowly took a dart from the pack, tested the sharpness of the tip and adjusted the flight. With another glance at me, he eased himself off his stool and stepped up to the mark.

'Double sixteen?'

'Ay.'

You could see by the way he took up his stance that he was an experienced player and must have been a good one. He stood slightly sideways, his weight evenly balanced on both feet, his wrist loose, upper arm steady, the dart at eye level. He adjusted his position slightly, carefully took aim and threw with a clean, smooth, sure movement.

The dart seemed to be heading straight for the target. Double sixteen. But it clipped the wire and the three of us hadn't even time to open our mouths as it bounced against the backboard and somersaulted through the air, landing directly in the middle of the flaming log fire.

Daisy

Una Stothard Smith

HOW'S your mother, Daisy?' Everybody asked after her mother. 'Nicely, thankyou. I've a nice little bit of fish to poach for her tea. She'll like that.'

Arthur sometimes came for his tea as well. Always on a Saturday. Oh, there was nothing to it. Daisy was fifty and she'd never married, but Arthur was too much of a gentleman to take advantage of that. His wife was very poorly and he needed a bit of fresh company now and then, that's all. He worked so hard. Poor Arthur. He was their firm's accountant and responsibility is a heavy burden. Such a shame his wife was ill. He needed looking after.

Daisy went round to Arthur's on a Saturday afternoon, when he was at the match. She took a duster and spent some time shining the place up for him. It didn't do her any harm and Phyllis was glad of it. My goodness, she only crocheted pillowslip edging if she didn't go to Arthur's. She had a lovely tension. Her mother said she had lovely tension.

Daisy would have been glad to do more but he never asked. It wouldn't have been proper. Dear Arthur. Always such a gentleman. She understood and, even though Phyllis said she must come more often, she still limited herself to Saturday afternoons when he wasn't there.

Daisy cooked a chicken every Saturday and, whilst the oven was on, she put in a couple of chocolate cakes.

'Nice bit of chicken, Daisy.' Her mother savoured it. 'Save some for Arthur. He might be coming for his tea. Such a nice gentleman. Pity about his wife.'

Daisy plumped up her mother's pillows. 'Don't worry about Arthur, Mother, there's plenty. And I've made a nice apple pie. He'll like that.'

She always took a tiny sliver with some apple sauce and a dainty piece of bread and butter for Phyllis. She gave it to her in bed after she had brought her some warm water and brushed her hair.

Phyllis knew Arthur called at Daisy's on a Saturday

after the match and she was glad he got a good meal at least once a week. He never stayed too long and it was kind of Daisy to take the trouble. Her mother was there. There was nothing to worry about. Not that Phyllis worried. She appreciated all Daisy did. They were good to her, both of them. She was a fortunate woman. She was very fortunate.

The only time she had ever doubted them was when Greta brought the news they had spent the whole day together on the office outing to Skegness.

Poor Phyllis was dying but she was taking her time about it. Daisy did everything she could to make her comfortable and towards the end it was really quite a strain. Her mother had become incontinent. Daisy was constantly dealing with sheets from one or the other of them and she stayed up half the night with Phyllis. Well, Arthur had to get his rest. She managed to get a few hours sleep in the evenings and went over to Arthur's to spend the small hours with Phyllis whilst he slept. She had to admit she sometimes nodded off during her lunch break, but these were difficult times for everybody.

There were pleasures too, of course. Saturday was her day off and it was then she baked cakes and cooked chicken and Arthur came for his tea. He only stayed a couple of hours, but it was all worth while. Everything seemed clean and well ordered.

Her mother could only manage a little chicken soup at lunch time. It made her feel impatient. She shouldn't be impatient with her mother. Not now, when she was so poorly.

There was a lot of space in her life after Phyllis died. Arthur didn't ask her to the funeral. She hadn't expected him to. All three of his sisters were there, and Greta went. But it wasn't as if she were a relation, or a neighbour. No, she really hadn't expected to be asked.

After the funeral, Arthur started coming home with her, on the same bus. He was a lonely man. They all ate a meal together and Daisy subsidised the housekeeping from her savings so that she could get something a bit special for Arthur. She liked to give him the best. He was such a nice person. She couldn't ask for a better.

She told him he must keep on bringing his washing. 'I wash every day for mother.'

But she did her own on a Sunday morning before church and she put Arthur's in with hers. It pleased her to think of his pyjamas tumbling round with her underwear. She even put a new crocheted edge on her underslip. Arthur had nice winceyette pyjamas. Warm to touch. It all seemed as it should be.

He came a lot for a few months. He stayed longer on Saturdays and he always called Mondays to pick up his laundry. There was a comfort in it, like being wrapped in cotton wool.

But after her mother died, although he still called to drop off his washing, he didn't stay. Daisy made a meal as usual but Arthur was seldom there to eat it. Such a waste.

When she asked him to come more often, he said he didn't want the neighbours to talk. Odd. She hadn't thought about it like that. But then, he was such a gentleman. She shouldn't have said it. It made here feel ashamed. As though she had suggested something improper.

Daisy put her mind to her place and started to crochet a bedspread. She had plenty of bedspreads but it gave her something to do and she worked her dreams into every stitch. She saw Arthur at the office of course, but he was a busy man nowadays. Well, he had the house to look after, hadn't he?

For some reason, she couldn't talk to him like she used to do. She wanted to. But something was different. She wasn't sure what it was, nor how it happened.

One day she made a simple remark about the weather and Arthur hadn't replied.

'Don't you think so, Arthur?'

He still didn't answer.

'Arthur...?'

He wasn't concentrating.

'Arthur, it looks like rain. Why don't you answer?'

She knew straight away she had gone too far. Her voice had sounded reproachful.

Arthur huffed. 'Didn't need an answer, did it?'

She knew it didn't. She knew very well. She had been so stupid.

Since then, the only times she saw him were before the match Saturday and on Monday when he picked up the ironing. She felt like a charwoman and hated herself for thinking so. She wanted to put things back together again but it was impossible. Arthur was unapproachable. He said hardly anything and his visits were as brief as they could be.

The girls at the office chattered. 'Arthur Penhalligon has a lady friend.'

They were like birds twittering over bacon rind. Daisy blushed and went on with her work.

Then it became clear they were not talking about her. It was somebody else. This woman, they said, was a floosie and man-fond. She didn't believe it. It couldn't be true.

Her heart started to thump and she felt the room was caving in around her. She went to the cloakroom and had a drink of water.

She began to suffer from indigestion and her appetite had gone. It was worse at nights: this hammering in her chest and the breathlessness. The doctor said it was the after effects of her mother's death and that she would get over it. The palpitations were from an over-active adrenaline gland, he said, and it would all pass. But it didn't.

On Saturday, her heart was in her mouth in case he didn't come. Grumbling bile rose into her throat and scoured her oesophagus until she was sick. She fell asleep on the settee in exhaustion and when she wakened, it was evening. Arthur had not been.

The next Saturday he stayed away, and the next. He was not coming any more. She sensed it. She pushed the thought away. It was not so. At work he always gave her a polite nod. He was so polite. She should never have criticised him. That stupid remark. So short tempered. She had no consideration for other people. She wished with all her heart she could relive the incident. She felt absolutely worthless. She didn't deserve anybody as decent as Arthur.

Then it was her birthday and the office staff gave her a

card. They had all signed it - including Arthur.

When she got home, she found a present on her window sill. It was a plant, a kind of daisy: her namesake. There was no card. No note to say who had brought it. The plant had been put on her window between the two sea-shells she had treasured ever since the office outing to Skegness. Who had brought it? She sought in her mind, pushing away the obvious. She would not admit even to herself who it might be - no, there was no card. Who would give her a birthday present?

She had to find out. She had to be sure.

She set about asking people. Nobody gave the right answer. She telephoned people she hadn't seen for years. She asked colleagues and they were embarrassed because they felt it ought to have been them.

But it wasn't. It wasn't anybody. Daisy knew it wouldn't be. But she went on asking all the same.

It became a password at work. 'Who sent Daisy the daisy?' they sang at her, and 'Daisy has an admirer.' She smiled at that. It made her feel better.

The weeks went by. The wondering - or was it the hoping? - had settled the unbearable panic attacks. Her last thoughts at night were about the daisy, and in the morning before her eyes opened she was filled with hope.

One morning she found some of its leaves had been eaten. She washed them gently and inspected her plant. There, winding itself round and round and hanging by a fragile thread, was a caterpillar turning itself into a chrysalis. It was an added charm. The plant had taken on a character of its own. It was family.

Then Greta called one Saturday morning. They chattered over a coffee.

'Have you ever seen a chrysalis, Greta? Look, I have one on my daisy.' And because the daisy was synonymous with the old question, she said: 'I had it on my birthday and I still don't know who sent it.'

'Don't you? Why, *I* know.'

Daisy felt a thump of apprehension hammer her chest. Not wanting her question to be answered, she had, nonetheless, implied she did, and Greta was always the first to tell whatever she knew.

'Why, yes,' Greta went on, 'Arthur!'

Daisy's heart jumped into her throat and started to throb, fast. Then it was true! What she had not dared to hope was true! She wished Greta would go away now. She wanted to nurse the thought in silence.

But Greta stayed. She had to lick round the pot.

'Yes, they had four plants when they called at our house. One for her, his fancy woman I mean, and one for each of his sisters. I told them it was no use taking one to their Madge's because they'd gone to Canada for a month. I thought they might have left it for me, but they didn't. I don't mind so much, now I know they've given it to you.'

Daisy couldn't speak. She was holding herself across her middle.

She turned away from Greta and walked to the window, still holding on to the pit of her stomach. She didn't know where she hurt most. Her skin hurt and pain squeezed its way through her pores. She swayed and grasped the sill for support.

She didn't know how long she stayed there, leaning against the window, rocking herself.

She didn't know when she realised the sun was too bright, or that Greta had left. She didn't know the chrysalis had changed, or what it meant.

Daisy saw, and did not see, the cocoon break open and the insect, ugly, wet and newborn, drying itself in the sun.

It opened its wings and their fluttering came within her vision. Its brilliance made her look at a world she no longer wanted to see. Tears smarted behind her eyes. They fell of their own accord. Silently, and without effort.

She cried - alone - at a butterfly, and she didn't even know its name.

Empires
Jim Wilson

THE Sowerby Bridge bus was standing outside the Volunteer Arms in Copley, filling up with schoolkids. The sensible thing would be to get on. I was late for work and the sack was hanging over me by a thread of frayed patience. But a blustery April fools' day of fractured seasons was rattling the green elders overhead and I just couldn't resist a walk along the Calder and Hebble Canal bank.

I joined the towpath behind the Volunteer and wove my way around the muddy edges of the double-glazed puddles that had frozen, melted and frozen again in the false starts of March. Too late I remembered the hole in my shoe.

I dawdled past Copley village with its great church of St Stephen set apart in a sad, damp birch wood. I lingered in the warmth from a little smelter near the canal and watched two schoolboys squatting on planks by a muddy pool. They fished for tadpoles by flooding jam jars. By then I was really late and had to step it out and start thinking up excuses.

Beyond the railway viaduct at the edge of the village, the towpath ran straight and open. I settled into a brisk march. Ahead was an iron bridge. An old man was scaling its stairs from the opposite bank, his dog already halfway across, hoovering the damp boards with its nose. By the time the old man reached the span, his dog was on my side of the canal and limping towards me, nosing half-heartedly into icy puddles.

In the middle of the bridge, the old man stopped and looked around. Although I was a hundred yards off, I knew he had spotted me and that he had made up his mind to intercept me. Unsociably, I accelerated. So did the old man.

I walked as quickly as I could, given the need to avoid puddles and look nonchalant, but by the time I reached the bridge, the only way to avoid him was to take flight.

He was standing on the towpath, stretching theatrically. When I got there, he was kneading the small of his back with his fists and letting out a moaning whistle.

'Bugger me,' he groaned with a smile, 'them bloody steps.'

Then, flicking a beer can skilfully into the canal with the tip of the stick, he stepped along beside me. 'Jip!' he called. The dog fell in, sniffing at my heels to make up a trio strolling unhurriedly to Sowerby Bridge. I was hopelessly late for work.

'You're late today,' the old man observed.

This was my chance. I could say 'Yes, excuse me,' and stride on, or I could ask him how he knew. I resigned myself to a late start.

We walked on together and I sneaked some snap shot glances of him. About average height, slight build, quite nimble. No need for the walking stick gripped in his blue-veined worker's hand which he used to slay dock leaves in the hedge. Cleanly dressed in cheap clothes a decade behind the fashion. A clash of beige and maroon. A widower, I presumed.

'I'm a bit late meself this morning,' he tried again before tromboning down a great broccoli-coloured nose into a handkerchief. 'Bugger it,' he continued, flourishing the rag and stowing it in his jacket pocket, 'I've nowt to hurry for. Not any more.' And he sniffed. His English blue eyes, stoically dry, searched me up and down. He was quite bald but wore no hat. He seemed painfully vulnerable.

'How do you know I'm late?'

He sprang alongside me, triumphantly decapitating a wild raspberry cane. 'Aha!'

At least we were moving at a good pace - till his stick sprang up across my chest like a barrier.

'See them? There.' He was pointing at a sandy bank opposite where a row of hawthorns leaned into the water. 'There. Look, there!' And he screwed his stick into the air in frustration at my obtuseness. 'Them holes.'

'Oh, yes, I see.'

There were three deliberate holes drilled in the sandbank. I needed to convince him I had seen them by pointing them out and counting them aloud. Then he lowered his stick and let me pass.

'Kingfishers' nests, them,' he said. 'Beautiful. Blue. Blue as ...' and he tried to tease the word out of the air with his cold fingers, '...green. Like flashes of lightning. Beautiful. Most beautiful thing on the canal. Sapphires. Like sapphires.

Keep it to yourself though. You never know.' He touched the side of his nose. 'Jewel thieves.'

I wondered if he was mad.

'Jip!' The dog stopped nosing in a tin can and loped behind us.

'This is where I worked,' he said, waving his stick over the wire works in its morning mist of steam and sulphuric acid. 'I started there,' he prodded his stick over the hedge into a warehouse of rusting coils, 'straight after I was demobbed. Thirty-eight year I did there. Retired just before the redundancies started. Got sod all. Story of my life, that is. Be my bloody epitaph. Harold Sutcliffe - got sod all.'

The idea seemed to please him.

'Now then, Arthur!' he shouted at a man hunched miserably over the wheel of a forklift truck, squirming through a muddy yard carrying quoits of wire.

'Now then, Harold. Come to gloat, have you?'

The old man beamed with delight and raised himself up for a sergeant major's holler. 'Get yer back into it, you idle sod!' He smiled at me like a father and strode on, taking the lead.

'Of course, all this,' and he waved an arc over the misty shambles of broken mills and corrugated lean-tos, 'belonged to the Sternes. Laurence Sterne lived here with his uncle.'

I was puzzled. 'Laurence Sterne?'

'Aye, the Tristram Shandy man. D'you want a spice?'

He handed me a bag of sticky sherbet lemons, then took one himself and threw one to the dog, who caught it in snapping jaws and crushed it with a curled lip.

We passed the wireworks and were walking through a graveyard of fallen mills. Dead, but still haunted by the wild satanic energy that had once driven them mercilessly round and round. Broken squares of stone filled with mounds of soft earth and willowherb. Rusty pivots for vanished doors. Rails for trucks turned turtle to die. Half-chimneys of cold furnaces. A warehouseful of coltsfoot and another of primroses.

'Up there, up Norland,' said the old man, nodding at a few houses on the valley side, 'Wordsworth wrote that Lucy Gray poem - *The storm came down before its time*,' he quoted. And then, pointing back to the opposite bank. 'My father worked there. They made finished cashmere,' he said proudly. 'Did the lot: sorting, combing, slubbing, spinning, weaving, carbonising - the lot. You won't find many places like that now. Eddlestones maybe, but that's all.'

'Course, my father was a loom tuner like my grandfather. Now he *did* earn some brass, lad, did my grandfather. Before the Great War. Here, listen.' He tapped me on the shoulder and pointed to his bald head so that I wouldn't miss the point. 'He'd come home paydays with a five pound note in his cap. That was a lot of money. Loom tuners could name their own price then. Good union, of course. Bosses needed them. Whole place buggered if the looms weren't tuned right.'

The old man speared a tumbling carrier bag and tossed it over his shoulder to the wind.

'My father never earned many fivers though. Looms changed. Tuners weren't needed. He came down to a twister, then a weaver. And that's how he retired. He got sod all too. It could be the family motto.'

This afterthought struck him as funny and he laughed until his eyes ran with tears. He coughed up a gob and spat it into the hedge. 'Oh dear,' he said and held his whole chest in a hand's span. He drew in a large sob of breath. 'Oh dear.'

'Mind you,' he said, trying to give the impression that it was adequate compensation, 'my Ashley's doing well. Oh yes. He's an accountant down in London. Money!' He shepherded the dog aside with his stick so that he could get close enough to whisper. 'He's got a house, cost a hundred thousand pound, in Luton. Now then.'

We walked on in silence for a while and then he ticked off Ashley's riches on the fingers of his hand. `Two cars he's got, flat in the Canaries, boat, caravan, the kids have tellies in their bedrooms.' He shook his head in bewilderment. 'I only hope it lasts, lad.'

'Over there.' He pointed to a charred mill on the opposite bank, with tongues of soot licking out of the tops of the windows. It had recently been torched for an insurance job. 'That's where my Annie worked before we were wed. There must have been two hundred lasses worked there before the War. Some lovely lasses too. Oh dear.' He took out his ragged handkerchief again, dried his eyes and blew his nose. 'Oh dear. Silly old bugger.' He stiffened his sinews and tried a few military steps but it was no use. The memory had its claws in his heart.

'I met her in Scarborough, last Wakes before the War. We walked out along the foreshore and onto the cliffs. We forgot all about time. I missed my chara and had to get on hers. Sat at her feet all the way home. More beer went down my neck than throat that trip. Oh dear.' He laughed a small, tearful giggle. I was frightened he would break down and kept a cautious couple of steps behind him. But he went on absently, half talking to himself, half talking to me over his shoulder.

'There's so many...' He shook his stick in front of him like a mine detector, looking for the word, '...*things* around now. So many... *things*.' He stopped suddenly and turned round to face me, his stick clasped under his arm and both his broken hands held like a begging bowl. 'We had nowt when we were wed, son. Me and Annie.' And he nodded into his empty hands for me to see for myself. 'Nowt!'

He moved on, shaking his head and still searching for words with his stick. 'We were wed when I came home on leave before going to Egypt. Embarkation leave it were called. And we moved into a house in King Cross with a bed and a table and four chairs. And that were it, lad.'

He stopped again, gripped my arm and pointed out a domestic rubbish tip down the embankment. 'There.' He nodded to the tip and smiled, as if he had found something he had been looking for. He pulled me closer to him so that we squinted along the line of his pointing stick.

'We were wed in '41.' He clamped his stick under his arm again and held up all his fingers for calculating. '1941, right.' He elbowed me lightly in the ribs to make sure I was paying attention. 'There'd been a Labour government in two years before we could afford a bit of carpet for the front room. Now then.' He nodded intensely at the rubbish tip, thinking out the words. 'And there, look!' A piece of rich red carpet spread lumpily over one of the mounds of rubbish. He held up six fingers. 'Six years before we got a bit of carpet for our front room. And there, look!'

He had made his point and it appeared to console and drain the tension from his body. He grasped his stick again and took a swipe at a magazine turning over its own pages on the towpath. It went flying onto the tip.

'Jip!' he called.

We started to make good time. Past a flat cindered area of sinking railway lines and scattered sleepers. Past great elm buffers, bolted together but rotting; the end of a line. Past mill walls with daffodils opening in their lee. Past outhouses and piles of stones beyond guessing, all covered with the chilly optimism of a creeping spring.

Still moving briskly, we ducked under the low bridges at Mearclough, past the raging weir on the Calder below us, around the railed-off, redundant gas works, past the squealing, clanking scrapyard whose nuts and bolts escape through its wire fencing and are trodden into the cinders of the towpath. And so into Sowerby Bridge basin.

There is a stone and iron-ringed peninsula of coveted berths here where shining cruisers roll gently on the black water. We stopped by a modern footbridge that vaults onto the peninsula and carries the towpath into Wharf Street. The old man leaned over the bridge's rail, swinging his stick and spitting absently onto the water.

'Look at that,' he said, pointing at a rich man's yacht in the basin, for sale at fifty thousand pounds. 'Look at that! How can anyone have so much brass to spare? Fifty thousand bloody pounds for a bloody boat to laik on.' He cut diagonal slashes across the whole scene with his stick, like a man trying to destroy an offensive picture.

'Ach!' He scraped the mud from his instep on the edge of the footbridge and changed the subject. 'Never mind, I've got a holiday lined up for Spring Bank. I'm going away with my boy and his family. Seaside. Proper bucket and spade job.' He blew his nose and smiled with satisfaction.

'Scarborough?' I asked in a flash of inspiration.

'Nay, Lanzarote,' he said. 'Warmer.' And, pointing at the northern sun that would never come to much, he crossed the bridge into Wharf Street.

'Jip!' he called.

Dolly At The Wedding

Gareth Martin

DEAR Betty,

Just a line or two to keep you up to date on what's been happening round here since your move. How is Cleveleys? I hope Vernon's skin has cleared up with the sea air. All those nasty flakes and scabs must have played havoc with your hoover.

Well, of course, the big news is the wedding of Mrs Pipe's boy Duane to the Beasley girl at St Lukes on Saturday, and not a day too soon, if you catch my meaning. I'm sure her family had given up hope of her ever catching a man; she's such a plain girl and so, well, robust. Our Trevor took her out once when they were teenagers. He took her to a rugby match and the man on the gate let them in free - he thought she was one of the visiting players! Anyway, she's put a lot of weight on recently, which accounts for the engagement only lasting a fortnight.

We got to the church early because I can't bear the thought of arriving late and giving all those people chance to stare at you as you scurry to a seat at the back. (If there's any staring to be done, I want to be doing it.) I was wearing a rather smart bottle green outfit I got from our Sharon's catalogue. They certainly seem to skimp on material in the fashion industry today, and I can only thank my mother for instilling in me the necessity of a sturdy foundation garment at all times. The usher asked us which side? And that posed the first problem as we've known both of them since they were knee-high to a dolly-blue but I noticed the bride's mother was wearing pink so we sat on the groom's side so we wouldn't clash.

Poor Mrs McVie sat next to me with Mr McVie, who was wearing a ridiculous tartan bow-tie. He will cling on to the illusion of being Scottish when poor Mrs McVie confided in me years ago that the furthest north he had ever been was to Redcar Races on the British Legion outing. There was a very respectable turn-out and I haven't seen as many people in church since the first Sunday after that handsome curate ran off with Ethel from the flower shop. I always said that woman would end up in the News of the World.

When the Wedding March struck up, everyone turned to watch the bride walk up the aisle on the arm of her father but, due to Mr Beasley being a bit unsteady on his feet for some reason, it was the other way round. Poor Mrs McVie said she looked a picture and I thought yes; painted by Van Gogh on one of his bad days. The dress was a very full, lacey construction, which, the bride's mother told me later, had been made by Normanton Nuptials and was in the Victorian style. I resisted the temptation to comment that it must have been a rush job as they'd put the bustle in the front. The colour, she said, was champagne-cream, which to me resembled nothing more than old net curtains - but at least she didn't wear white, which would have been stretching credibility to absolute breaking point, in my opinion.

The bridesmaids were the bride's sisters who wore yellow. They had little head-dresses of forget-me-nots which looked out of place perched on top of the youngest one's Mohican hair-do. Two little mucus factories in blue sailor suits carried the train, one of them wiping his nose on it at times.

The service went off quite well - the only sticky moments were Duane's hesitancy with the responses, which he managed to get through with a little encouragement from the bride's elbow, and the vicar glancing worriedly at Mr Beasley and rushing to get to the end before he fell over - not the vicar, Mr Beasley. Our Trevor was the best man (him and Duane are members of the same pigeon club) and he did his little bit beautifully. Of course, when the vicar asked for the ring, he made a play of not being able to find it, which some thought went on a little too long, but he took it out of his shoe in the end. He can always be relied on to add style to these things, can our Trevor.

Everyone gathered outside the church for photographs which were delayed because the bridesmaid with the

Mohican had gone missing. They eventually found her in the vestry but she couldn't be in the photos because somehow she'd managed to Superglue the hem of her dress to her nose and there was an unseemly show of unusual underwear. Put it this way, if the men of Grimsby had as many holes in their fish-nets, we'd all be eating Icelandic haddock.

The reception was held at the Inkerman Hotel in the Blue Room. Why they call it the Blue Room escapes me as everything in it is the same nicotine brown, even the curtains, but I suppose it must have been blue once. It was an odd way to begin a reception because the bride and groom were late. Duane had called in at home to check on his pigeons. When they arrived, instead of them greeting the guests, we stood in a line while they walked along shaking hands. It was like meeting the Queen and Prince Philip at the Royal Variety Performance.

They'd laid on a three course meal with wine and coffee. The waitress was Mrs Jowett from Enderby Street, the one who was so poorly that time. I haven't seen her since she came out of quarantine but I think she recognised me.

The soup was tomato and would have been okay if it had been as warm as the white wine. There was turkey or beef for the main course. I had beef because the turkey was sliced paper thin and in perfect circles. It looked like white Spam and, according to poor Mrs McVie, tasted like it too. Mind you, I hadn't much better luck with the beef which was tough and when I mentioned it to the manager later, he said: 'You must have got a bit where the shafts had been rubbing,' laughed and walked away.

To follow, there was 'fresh fruit salad' which would have done the man from Del Monte proud, but by this time I'd had a couple of Tio Pepes and a glass of wine and was starting to enjoy myself.

The speeches were a disaster except for our Trevor who stood up, read the telegrams, proposed a toast to the bride and groom and sat down without taking a breath; he's always been more of a thinker than a talker, has our Trevor. Mr Beasley had fallen somewhere and had a nasty gash on his forehead which was bleeding down his face and dripping off the end of his nose into his fruit salad. Poor Mrs McVie took the crepe bandage off her varicose ulcer and helped to wrap his head, but he couldn't be impressed upon to speak, which was probably for the best, really.

Mr Pipe, Duane's dad, who runs the local rugby team and whose sense of humour has always been questionable, stood up and said that he didn't look upon it as losing a son so much as gaining a prop forward, which caused some rumblings among the Beasley contingent - I suppose because they all play soccer.

The afternoon degenerated with more beer and Cherry B's until Mr McVie began to sing Loch Lomond with his head firmly planted in Mrs Beasley's bosom and I decided it was time for home and a sleep before the evening's festivities.

The evening do was held in the upstairs room at the British Legion. There was a disco, which upset me straight away as I'd promised myself a 'Gay Gordons' before the night was out, but I took two distalgesics and an advocaat and decided to grin and bear it. Poor Mrs Mcvie joined us at our table with Mr McVie, who'd been home and changed into full Scottish regalia, kilt, sporran, the lot.

The wedding presents were stacked up on a table down the side of the room and they'd done very nicely really. Someone had bought them a lovely hostess trolley but I mentioned to poor Mrs McVie that if the daughter cooked anything like her mother, it would get very little use. It's all baked beans and oven chips in their house, everyone knows it. Poor Mrs McVie said that she'd heard Duane talking to our Trevor and he'd said the trolley would do very well for incubating his pigeon eggs.

Someone had given them three flying ducks for the wall and I swear they were the same set that have turned up at every wedding round here for thirty years. Even the wrapping paper was the same. Those ducks have seen more places than any of Peter Scott's migrating mallards.

We gave them a melamine salad set with handles in the shape of Skipton Castle, and I was pleased to see they got pride of place on top of the hostess trolley, but I was a little worried in case they got pinched.

There was a finger buffet on one end of the present table consisting of curled-up sandwiches and soggy vol-au-vents filled with thick green stuff that someone said was creamed mushroom. The centrepiece was a very sad looking Black Forest gateau. Mrs Pipe came over and told us to help ourselves to the food and apologised that the prawns had been eaten off the top of the vol-au-vents. She said that the cost of the day had nearly crippled them, as the Beasleys couldn't contribute due to Mr Beasley's status as an undischarged bankrupt, but at least he was buying his own beer. He was sitting in the corner with poor Mrs McVie's bandage round his head and looking quite dazed.

By this time, the younger ones were all dancing to what Mr McVie said was Rock and Roll but when the bride took to the floor, there seemed to be a lot more roll than anything else. I managed to get a word with the bride between pints of Snakebite and I asked her if she and Duane were going on honeymoon. She told me they'd booked in at the Bella Nova in Cleethorpes, and when I asked her if she was having the Bridal, she said: 'No, I'll just hang on to his ears till I get used to it', which goes to show what's going on in the minds of young people today.

Mind you, I think it's the example set by some of the older ones which causes all the problems. Some of those who are old enough to know better were taking part on the dance floor by now, and my attention was drawn to Mr McVie who was doing the Highland Fling. No mean feat this, considering his face was stuck in Mrs Beasley's bodice once more. Anyway, she didn't seem to mind and was cutting a healthy rug herself, but the same could not be said for *Mr* Beasley, who had come alive and was lurching across the room towards the couple. When he reached them, he made no more to-do than aim what I think is termed a ferocious right cross at Mr McVie's jaw. Unfortunately, the headlong rush across the room had dislodged his bandage, which fell over his eyes as he came within distance. The blow missed Mr McVie by a mile, who jigged on regardless, but hit Duane, who was making his way across the floor with a huge wedge of Black Forest Gateau.

Duane went down like a poleaxed ox, landing at the feet of the dancing Mr McVie who, oblivious to all around him, stepped into the cake and flew into the air, landing on his back, kilt and sporran round his chin.

Two of life's great mysteries were solved for me that night. The first was what Scotsmen wear under their kilts, and the second was why poor Mrs McVie is so called. How that woman must have suffered, poor dear.

Well, the fighting started with both families going at it hammer and tongs and we beat a hasty retreat, followed closely by our Trevor and Sharon, I'm glad to say. He's always been more of a lover than a fighter, has our Trevor.

The latest news is that Mr McVie has moved in with Mrs Beasley and Mr Beasley hasn't had much to say about it considering that when the bride saw him banjo Duane, she countered with a left hook which saw her father into intensive care, and the bride remanded in custody for malicious wounding. Oh, and I saw Mrs McVie in the High Street the other day. She had a smile on her face and a spring in her step for the first time in years, bless her.

Well, Betty, we may be poor but we do see life. That's all for now, give my love to Vernon and tell him to keep up with the Calamine.

Love, Dolly

PS. I'll send you the melamine salad set with handles shaped like Skipton Castle. I know you like that sort of thing.